RENEGADE RIVER

Jim Bayles blames the Garnett outlaws for the disappearance of his brother Hector, a federal officer. But when he wounds Charlie Garnett, his errant cousin, he finds he's no nearer the truth, the wound having caused amnesia. However, sided by Charlie, Jim repeatedly clashes with the gang. They're forced to cross the Rio Grande to Mexico, where they learn what really happened. Then, facing the final lethal clash, Charlie — his mind restored — must decide between his outlaw partners and Jim . . .

DAVID BINGLEY

RENEGADE RIVER

Complete and Unabridged

LINFORD
Leicester

First published in Great Britain in 1973

First Linford Edition
published 2010

British Library CIP Data

Bingley, David, *1920* –
  Renegade river. - -
  (Linford western library)
  1. Western stories.
  2. Large type books.
  I. Title II. Series
  823.9'14–dc22

ISBN 978–1–44480–472–0

Published by
F. A. Thorpe (Publishing)
Anstey, Leicestershire

Set by Words & Graphics Ltd.
Anstey, Leicestershire
Printed and bound in Great Britain by
T. J. International Ltd., Padstow, Cornwall

This book is printed on acid-free paper

1

The ghost town on Fall Creek, on the west side of the Pecos River in south-west Texas, had as many small nerve-shattering noises as every other empty skeleton of a town, even at three o'clock in the afternoon. In the ten years since a failure in a local mine had brought about the settlement's decline, birds of all descriptions and many small animals had gradually moved in and made it their home.

Ordinary humans shunned the place, thinking it a town of ill-luck, a spot to be avoided. Year by year, the boards had peeled and the timbers swelled, so that now, not many doors would close properly and the breezes which made them swing and creek moaned through window spaces long devoid of glass.

On this particular day, Ghost Town Creek was having itself a ball: at least, that was the private view of Jim Bayles as he sat on high ground with his broad back against a thin plank wall exterior pitted with knot holes. The main items of his trade, namely a thick writing pad and a couple of well-sharpened pencils, had just been discarded in favour of his spyglass which was now placed to his right eye and trained on a building lower down on the other side of what had been the main street.

The building in question had long since lost its false front on a stormy winter's night, and now, the four men who had ridden in with care and placed their tired bodies on the rotting floorboards were clearly visible to the unknown watcher on the hill.

Jim was very excited about his observations because he knew the quartet, even though they had been out of circulation for some time and their trails had never crossed. He knew without a doubt three out of the four from photographed faces on reward notices. They were the Garnett gang of outlaws. Two years earlier the Garnetts had been the most notorious outfit of their kind between the Texas section of the great Rio Grande River and its formidable tributary, the Pecos.

No wonder Jim Bayles was excited. His broad, capable hands shook a little as he held the glass to his eye and checked the faces, one after another. Many a bounty-hunter with the nerve to tackle that quartet single-handed in that isolated place would have taken that particular afternoon as part of one of his great days.

Jim slowly licked his lips and blinked often. Bounty-hunting was not his job in life, although he had been partly instrumental in bringing about this meeting between himself and the undesirable outlaw gang.

Jim was a travelling journalist. He travelled with his pad and pencils. He lived by putting words together, describing places and people and writing down interviews. The telegraph system made it possible for him to get his material to many towns with the minimum delay and, because he was fairly well known, he made a reasonable living.

In appearance he was worth a second glance. His tall, straight-backed figure hinted that he was used to horses, had done military service and that he was a man of some authority. At thirty, his black hair — worn long — looked a whole lot darker than the flat-crowned dusty stetson which he wore well forward on his forehead, close above his straight brows. Long tapering sideburns outlined the cheeks and upper jaws of a strong face which boasted a pair of very steady blue eyes, a slightly Roman nose and a neat firm mouth.

Abruptly, the watcher lowered his glass. He began to breathe as though he had been holding his breath. By searching through old reports and visiting the locations which the gang had been known to use, he had brought about a meeting two years after they had apparently ceased to operate.

He had every reason to be excited, particularly as this meeting could further a personal scheme very close to his heart. He wanted information from them, but he could hardly walk out there into the main thoroughfare and explain that he knew who they were and expect them to answer his questions.

Any such foolhardy move could only achieve a sudden death by lead poisoning from a group of outlaws who clearly would not want any of their plans for the future publicising. All he could do was challenge them in a way they understood. They would react in the only way they knew how and, with luck, he might be in a position to delay one of them sufficiently to get the information he wanted.

Even as he planned, he realised that his scheming was much nearer to his taking the law into his own hands than anything else he had done in his thirty years. During the war between the north and south, almost anything could have taken place, but in peacetime, even in a ghost town, with characters such as these, his plan could be described as a bloodthirsty one by anyone who happened along and bore witness to it.

And if his observations had served him correctly, there would be others along that way within the next hour or so. He took another quick look through the glass and decided that he was too far away to hit a moving target, in the event that the quartet suddenly decided to scatter.

If he was to carry out his scheme, he would have to go closer. That much was certain. He collapsed his glass, gathered up his weapons and set off, walking as quietly as possible and taking advantage of every bit of shade.

Some five minutes later, he entered the rear of a building on the near side of the main street which had once been two-storey offices. The warped stairs almost trapped him as he went up them, but he succeeded in extricating a foot as one gave way under him and arrived at the upper level intact, although he had added many more creaking sounds to those which the wind promoted.

Soon, he was kneeling in front of a window which faced the other frontless building across the street, with his well-oiled Winchester to hand and the brim of his hat pushed back. The critical time had arrived. The Garnetts were still sitting in the same positions. No one had attempted to sleep, but one cigar and two cigarettes had been lighted.

Clearly, they were entered upon a discussion of some importance.

Jim cleared his throat. 'Hey, you four men over there, can you hear me?'

The sudden and unexpected vocal challenge had tensed up the four seated men. All of them had reached for their guns, but this far there had been no other move.

'Who's a-callin' an' why don't you show yourself?'

7

The voice which had answered had a dry, brusque quality. Perhaps it was intended to disarm the unknown enquirer. Jim Bayles guessed rightly that it belonged to Matt Garnett, the gang leader, a man in his late thirties.

'My name wouldn't interest you boys,' Jim called back calmly. 'The fact is, I know who you are and the sort of record you have, so I'm bein' quite fair with you at the outset. Ain't that so?'

Again, the outlaws were slow to answer, but it was clear that Jim's line of approach had startled them. They had moved slightly further apart, staying low and turning their bodies towards the gaping front of the old saloon so that they could meet any sudden challenge in an instant.

At that time, the shadowy gloom of the old building protected them to some extent. Towards the rear, two glassless windows had been boarded up and the rear door had been given the same treatment. If they had to, they could get out without rushing through the front wall, but they needed time to force an exit through either the boarded door or the windows.

'Who do you suppose we are, stranger?'

'Matt Garnett and other members of the same gang that went to earth in these parts a couple of years ago.'

'We ain't all that good on old history, bein' travellin' gents. But say it happened to be true. What do you propose to do about it?'

'I'd be doin' the authorities a favour if I scattered you all, an' that's what I plan to do, Matt. So now you know. You can start comin' forward jest as soon as you're ready!'

One of the four fired a probing revolver shot towards one side of the open front wall. While the echoes were still punishing the rotting dry wood-work, another hand weapon sounded off, this time aimed towards the other side of the gaping opening. A rifle pumped two shells into the lower storey of the building where Jim was holed up.

It was time he tried to move them.

He lined up his Winchester on a spot between one of the rear windows and the sealed door of the saloon. His shot was well timed, because one of the four had crawled back and was checking up on the soundness of the bolt holes.

'I said to come out by the front,' Jim reminded them. 'It ain't good manners to go any other way. Besides, that way we wouldn't get acquainted.'

Seconds slipped by during which another man, thinking he was possibly hidden from the marksman, crawled to the other window and reached up. Jim blasted off at him, and in so doing removed the fellow's stetson purely by chance.

Now they were taking more notice of him. They would have reasoned that he was no lawman: that he was almost certainly on his own. Furthermore, it was unlikely that he could wing more than one of them if they all came out together and put up plenty of covering fire.

Jim had only one move left to him before the rush came. He ducked below the window frame as revolver and rifle bullets probed his hiding place and moved on his knees to another window about five yards away. A partition between two offices which had disappeared made this possible.

As the leaden slugs ripped into the woodwork, Jim experienced the peculiar thrill which gunfire gives to any man who has ever lived through an intense barrage in wartime. Bullets, he thought, engendered gambling with lives in a quick game of chance in which there was no neutral banker.

The rush came without warning. Jim rose to his feet, telling himself all over again what he had planned to do. In his earlier days, he had always shot to kill. That was the way of things in wartime, but now he had to shoot to wound: to leave one of his enemies on the field of battle, to be interrogated later.

His first shot was aimed at the legs of the barrel-chested man with the ginger moustache. Seemingly, he missed, because the fellow shifted his boots hurriedly and kept coming forward. Other bullets, hastily blasted from hand guns, failed to distract Jim as he lined up on another character seeking to make his exit by the same side.

This chap was shorter, with sloping shoulders. He seemed more uncertain of himself than the other, and younger, in spite of the small close-trimmed brown beard and moustache which met wide of his mouth. As the outlaw paused for a quick glance into the danger area, Jim lined up on him, panned his Winchester muzzle and squeezed.

Even as the bullet left the muzzle of his weapon, he was reflecting that he had attempted the almost impossible. This time he had not aimed low. His shell had been aimed high, in a careful effort to crease the runaway and deprive him of his senses. Almost at once, it became clear that he was on target. His victim paused, spun around and fell backwards, applying his hands to his head, having dropped his revolvers.

Already, one of the four was darting up the misshapen boards of the sidewalk. Two others followed. One of them paused to sight carefully at Jim's window and that, he surmised, was the time to improve his cover. He dropped into a prone position, noted that three or four more bullets came his way, and then started to think of his next move.

He got up a minute later, when all had gone quiet in regard to gunplay, and checked over the rear of the building. This one had another directly behind it, if he ever had to move quickly. Having precipitated trouble in such an isolated spot, he now had to be prepared for almost anything.

The previous night, he had slept out in the open. He knew that a party of surveyors, doing work for a railroad, had planned to take a close look at the ghost town that same afternoon, but he had had no serious contact with them and if they had decided to come a day later he was in serious trouble, because no one else was likely to come near a place which had been for so long deserted.

Serious trouble if the Garnetts counter-attacked.

They did. The wounded man stayed where he was, but the others patiently closed in upon the building from which the attack had been launched. A sudden sharp noise in the intersection near the offices warned Jim that he would probably be blasted if he attempted to leave by the rear door.

He backed away from the stairs. The rear window in the room he was occupying really consisted of a pair of french doors, with a narrow balcony outside. The balcony extremity was no further than six feet from the opposite window in the building behind. Furthermore, the other window was merely a hole in the wall. It had lost both glass and frame.

Two furtive whispers warned the

young journalist that he was almost hemmed in. If he did not want to make his stand in that building, it was time to go. One gunman was in the intersection. The other was making an Indian-like approach from the other side.

Jim listened. There was no sound to suggest the close proximity of horses. He had to fend for himself now. He checked over his gear and stepped through the french doors, measuring the distance between the balcony and the window in the other building with his eye.

He had a feeling that someone was eyeing him, or about to see him from some angle. This feeling jangled his nerves a little. On impulse, he fired two bullets from his .45. One at the corner next to the intersection, the other towards the opposite end of the block.

Having made his gesture, he sprang up on to the gallery rail with rather more force than was necessary. He had just time enough to adjust his leap and then he was in space, travelling on the effort made by one leg.

His hat seemed to flop on his head. Momentarily, the Winchester felt as though it would topple him sideways. And then he was across, with his boot heels just scraping the sill of the window as he passed through it. By tilting his head forward, he had kept his stetson and prevented a nasty blow on the forehead.

Breathing noisily with relief, he sank to the boards and stayed there, casting aside his shoulder weapon and the spyglass. He pulled off his hat, and massaged rather than rubbed his forehead and neck.

While he savoured the temporary relief, running footsteps negotiated the narrow space between the two buildings. Hand guns blasted through the rear windows on the ground floor of the edifice recently vacated. Two men moved into the office block, raced up the stairs and noisily proclaimed their disbelief when they found their enemy not there.

If Jim had acted out of character in precipitating the shooting match, he now called upon his reserves of patience and other useful traits to play for time and to outguess the outlaws.

A skylight permitted him another move. While the searching was continued over a wider area, he muscled his way through to the roof and settled himself down in the scant shelter of a sloping wooden protection, warped almost to the shape of a pagoda.

A full hour and a half dragged by with the Garnetts making no progress in their search. Shortly after that, the sound of several horses, moving together, came from the south-east. At that point, Matt Garnett decided that he had searched long enough for one elusive enemy.

He rode out with his two unscathed brothers, leaving another horse for the wounded man, in case he was able to ride and to slip away undetected.

Charlie Garnett was the man left behind. He was only a cousin to Matt and the other two, otherwise Matt would have thought twice about leaving him to fend for himself. Charlie was wounded and he was hurt, but Jim had achieved what he set out to do. He had creased the outlaw along the side of his left temple.

The puckered burn mark looked anything but pleasant, and Jim had experienced a few pangs of regret by the time the riding group came along and found him in the frontless saloon. Deputy Mick Dowell, a somewhat over-diligent peace officer from the county sheriff's office, dismounted hurriedly and came to stand behind Jim, who was then bathing the wounded man's head.

Dowell ignored Jim, staring at the other's face as though he took a lot of pride in knowing and apprehending wrongdoers. A wolfish sort of grin spread across his lean lined face as his memory went to work on the features. He dabbed touches of perspiration out of his greying fair moustache and sideburns.

'That there is one of the Garnett

boys. I don't recollect a picture out for him. I guess he must be the one called Charlie. Ain't that something, now?'

He turned, expecting Jim to exult over the new and exciting knowledge, but all he got was a nod. Instead of furthering the conversation, Jim stood up and moved to meet the leader of the four-man expedition, a tall, older person with a waxed grey moustache and rather piercing eyes. He had on a tall undented black stetson of expensive material and a tailored grey suit.

'You must be Major Hunt, the railroad surveyor, I think,' Jim began. 'I've heard about you in my travels. My name is Jim Bayles. I'm a journalist.'

The two men greeted each other without reserve, shaking hands warmly and at the same time examining each other openly and with frank admiration.

'Not James H. Bayles who writes the Westerner column in the *Blackrock Banner*?'

The conversation continued between the two men, while two assistant surveyors came up quietly in the background and Deputy Dowell tried hard to think of something to make it a three-cornered conversation. Again, his memory served his well. He came up behind the surveyor and interposed himself, pointing a crooked index finger at Jim.

'There was a famous man in my line, a federal deputy, mixed up with the Garnetts a couple of years back! Hector Bayles, his name was! He has to be your brother, an' you're takin' up where your brother left off!'

Jim tried to show a warmth he did not feel towards the deputy. He explained that his clash with the old gang of outlaws had not happened because he wanted to emulate his brother. Dowell, who had a way of putting himself into the middle of things, intimated that he would be only too glad to escort Charlie back to the sheriff's headquarters.

At this point, Jim's manner changed. 'I'm sure you have enough to keep you busy in your special assignment with the major, here. Me, I'll be takin' the wounded man in myself. He'll need a doctor before any peace office takes over. Rest assured, I'll be in full control.'

Major Hunt, who also had difficulty at times in keeping the pushing deputy in his place, warmed still further to Jim as the latter asserted himself. Between them, the surveyor's party help to hoist the wounded man into an old buckboard which still functioned and they rode to the edge of town to speed the departure of the conveyance pulled by two unaccustomed riding horses.

The wounded man was bandaged, unconscious and moaning quietly as the moving vehicle shook him.

2

Doctor Richard Mallin, M.D., looked older than his thirty-two years on account of his receding dark hair and the gold-rimmed spectacles which made his expression seem severe. He was a fairly tall man with a fresh complexion. A small black moustache balanced his immature baldness. This was one more feature which aged him.

Mallin had served in the same regiment with Jim Bayles during the war. What he had seen of carnage made him want to take up medicine and surgery. He was a very busy man, but not too busy to do an old friend a good turn, particularly when that old friend happened to call at his private house on the northern outskirts of Blackrock, a town situated to the south-west of Fall Creek and the ghost town.

By six o'clock the following evening,

Bayles and the wounded outlaw had been in the doctor's hands for just about one day. Mallin had come home from his extensive rounds an hour earlier, and the two of them, accompanied by Mrs Mallin, were enjoying a splendid three-course meal provided by the latter.

Mabel Mallin was a thoughtful, plump, strong-bodied woman of thirty-five who had trained on the east coast as a nurse before coming west and meeting up with her husband. She contrived to wait at table and at the same time take her own food, wearing for the occasion a neat black skirt and a white blouse, edged with lace at the neck. Her brown hair, pinned back in a bun, gave her a severe look which matched her sharp features.

The doctor came to the end of a brief recital of what he had done during the day, and inclined his head towards the spare bedroom, where Charlie Garnett had languished in a state of unconsciousness since his arrival.

Jim, who was busy with a piece of steak, shook his head.

Mrs Mallin, perceiving the trend of her husband's thoughts, cleared her throat and added: 'He looked as if he might regain consciousness a couple of times before noon, but since then he's slept soundly. He might go through the night like that.'

Dick Mallin was slow to answer. Jim felt his friend's eyes on him and knew a sharp pang of guilt. He renewed his interest in the food and complimented the woman, creating a small diversion of sorts. Some ten or fifteen minutes later, the food was consumed and the men moved into easy chairs, while the lady of the house removed the dirty dishes to the kitchen and closed the door behind her.

Mallin watched a thin plume of smoke go up from the bowl of his pipe. 'Jim, do you think the Garnetts disposed of your brother the other year? I know you were very devoted to him.'

'I don't rightly know the answer to

that, Dick,' Jim admitted. He rubbed his forehead which was wrinkled with a frown. 'It's not knowin' that makes me feel so bad. I need to find out, an' the only way I can do that is get the information from the outlaw family.'

'If, in fact, they had anything to do with his disappearance,' the doctor remarked mildly. 'I don't like the look of Garnett's head, where you shot him, but I suppose your aim was accurate if your intention was to render him unconscious to question him at a later date.'

Jim shifted uneasily, guessing at what the doctor was thinking behind his spoken words. 'I took a chance with that man's life, Dick, and I wouldn't argue otherwise. Maybe if I had to do again what I did in that ghost town I wouldn't be so successful. Maybe I wouldn't have a wounded man for you to attend to. I can only excuse myself by sayin' that most of the gang are still wanted by the law, dead or alive.'

Mallin's features reflected a lot of his

thinking. As he thought, he toyed with his pipe, tamping it down frequently and testing its drawing power. He was just beginning to get on Jim's nerves when Charlie Garnett uttered a pained cry. Both men stood up at the same time, and the kitchen door opened, revealing the housewife who was prepared to do anything her husband said.

Mallin waved her back into the kitchen. He gestured for Jim to follow him and went into the spare bedroom where the wounded man was writhing gently on the wide single bed and staring at the unfamiliar walls.

'Is your head painin' you?' Mallin asked, crouching over him.

'Something sure is, brother! How come did I get all these bandages? What's been happenin' to me? Where am I?'

'You're in the spare bed at my house. I'm Dr Mallin, of Blackrock. You got yourself involved in some shootin' the other day, over at a place the locals call

Ghost Town Creek. Does that ring a bell in your head?'

Charlie grimaced. After a short pause he nodded. And then his eyes were wide and he was examining the two men in the room with great interest. Jim moved a bowl of liquid closer to the bed and Mallin began to slowly strip off the bandages.

'You remember the events in Ghost Town Creek?' Mallin repeated.

The doctor was wondering just how much Charlie did remember, and whether he had any sort of an inkling that Jim Bayles was the fellow involved with the gang.

'I don't remember nothin', Doc, an' that's the truth. If I fooled you by noddin' jest now I'm sorry. I was noddin' because I do have bells, sort of, ringin' in my head. Tell me, is it a bullet wound of some sort?'

Mallin peeled off the rest of the bandaging and held Charlie's head lightly against the pillow. He frowned and the expression on his face galled

Jim, who was hovering behind him.

'It sure was a bullet wound, Charlie,' Mallin assured him. 'Right alongside of your left temple. A very delicate spot.'

Jim wanted to talk to break the tension building up inside him, but he was not sure what sort of a line to take with this Garnett whom he had captured, and who claimed not to remember anything.

'First off, Doc,' Charlie began, 'I'd like you to tell me my full name. An' when we've cleared that one, I'd be pleased to know how I was mixed up in that shootin' you spoke of.'

Mallin was bathing the wound by this time. Jim knew him well enough to know that Charlie was in for a lot of sympathy with him, on account of the wound, whereas he — Jim — was being regarded for the moment as a villain, the doer of the deed.

'I was there at the ghost town,' Jim informed him hurriedly. 'After the shootin' was over a peace officer happened along. He said your name was Charlie.'

'But what is my other name, amigo?' Charlie repeated patiently.

'Would you know it if you heard it?' Jim countered.

'Try me, try me,' Charlie almost pleaded. 'Would I keep askin' if I knew it? Would I?'

'Well, most of the other fellows who were doin' the shootin' were called Garnett. Does that name mean anything to you?'

'No, it doesn't,' the patient replied automatically. 'Now, do you have any other suggestions to make?'

'Have you heard of anyone called Bayles, for instance? Or Smith, or Hunt, or Dowell?'

'What does the name Mallin mean to you?' the doctor asked, as Jim appeared to run out of ideas.

'None of those names means anything to me, friend,' Charlie replied warily, 'but your suggestion, Doc. I know that. That's *your* name. You told me that jest a few minutes ago! So what is your friend called?'

'His name is Bayles, Jim Bayles. He was there when the shootin' occurred.'

Jim expected any second to be asked if he had done the shooting, but the patient had not this far moved around to that point of view.

'Jim was the fellow who brought you out of the town an' into Blackrock. He's quite anxious for you to get well as soon as possible.'

The underlying depths of feeling behind the doctor's remarks were, fortunately, lost on the suspicious patient. The doctor worked on the wound with a very light touch. As he did so, he talked about Blackrock in the hope that Garnett would remember something about it; something to start him remembering.

It occurred to the doctor that both he and Jim wanted the man's memory restored, but that their reasons were very different unless Jim was suffering rather belatedly from a touch of conscience. As the two-way talk between doctor and patient went on with no suggestion of a reaction from the stricken man, Jim began to feel out of place in the sick room.

Consequently, he manoeuvred himself towards the door. He wanted to recover his cigar and think out the implications behind Charlie's apparent loss of memory. Clearly, Dick would feel that the outlaw had been shot unnecessarily. In the doorway, Jim looked back. He wanted to ask all sorts of clinical questions about memory failure, but this was not the time.

'Hey, Jim, could I ask you one more question before you go through that door?'

Charlie had raised his head a little, as it was being bandaged.

Jim nodded, and Charlie said : 'Was I travellin' with you when you went along to that ghost town?'

The young journalist tried to hide the troubled look on his face as he shook his head. 'No, Charlie, before that occasion we had never known each other.'

Jim nodded and moved out into the big room where they had eaten their food. Five minutes later, the doctor joined him.

'Is he — is he startin' to remember, Dick?'

The professional man threw himself heavily into his chair. 'No, no signs at all. I know he's sincere, too. He really does not remember anything that happened to him before you shot him.'

Jim gestured with his hands. 'Is he likely to stay in that condition for any length of time?'

The doctor pushed his spectacles up on to his forehead and blinked at him several times. 'Amnesia, that's the techical name for loss of memory, is a very tricky thing. He'll pick up physically, all right, but his powers of recollection may remain impaired for the rest of his life.'

Jim revealed how much he was shocked by this pronouncement by half-rising out of his chair, and pointing with his cigar.

'On the other hand, the memory might be restored. It might return to him tonight, or tomorrow, next week or next month. And then again — '

'And then again he might never remember that he's a Garnett an' what happened to him,' Jim put in bitterly.

'I hope he won't have to suffer long,' Mallin said calmly, as his wife came in to join them.

The doctor left her to judge for herself what state the patient was in. She sat down with some knitting and quietly began to take in the conversation, occasionally shooting a quick glance at one or the other of them.

'Dick, it's painfully clear that your sympathy is with the patient. *I* hope he gets well soon, too, and for the same reason as yourself. But I'd like to remind you that there are other ways of sufferin' that don't always bring the sufferer to a doctor's couch.

'I've been sufferin' in the mind ever since my brother disappeared in the wake of those — those Garnetts! I jest don't know if he's alive! It might well be that Charlie Garnett was the one who shot my brother to death! Can you understand that?'

'I can understand that, Jim,' Mallin returned in a neutral voice. 'You've been troubled in your mind because of uncertainty. It's made you do what you felt you had to do. But face it, old friend, you can't go around shootin' unconscious all the possible people who might have shot at and wounded your brother! You do see that, don't you?'

Jim gripped the arms of the chair, hoping that Mrs Mallin could not know the tension that was in him.

'Dick, I know that to a man in your profession I did wrong back there in the ghost town by deliberately shootin' this man! I know that, an' seein' as how I'm usin' your hospitality I don't feel good about it. Things haven't turned out the way I wanted them. Not at all, they haven't!

'But if fate had decreed otherwise, I might have been a bounty-hunter when

I found the gang located in that derelict place, and then, so help me, Charlie and probably other members of the family could have been shot dead! The reward is paid for this particular group of outlaws, dead or alive!'

'Please calm down, if you can, Jim. I know your line of reasoning. I take life very seriously myself. You know I do that. I went along to the peace office this morning an' got permission to look over some old reward notices. I found three for the Garnett gang, but this boy, Charlie, didn't have his picture in the drawer. There was no reward offered for him on any charge.'

Jim started to thump the arm of the chair.

'All right, all right,' Mallin resumed. 'I know that doesn't mean he's without guilt! But it jest goes to show we can't afford to let our emotions run away with us. Do you agree or not?'

Jim agreed at once, and shortly afterwards he slipped out of doors on the pretext of going for a walk.

3

After that rather grim evening on the day when Charlie recovered consciousness, Jim Bayles took a grip of himself. When the issue was a worthwhile one, he normally had all the patience necessary to cope with whatever ensued. Over Charlie Garnett he had rather let himself down. Now, however, he intended to make amends; show Richard Mallin that he still had as much patience and determination as he had shown in wartime conditions.

Two days later, the amnesia still had its grip upon Charlie, and although he was physically a whole lot fitter and quite curious about himself and everything about him, he was still confined for part of the day to his room or the building.

Some quirk of conscience made Jim spend as little time as possible in the sick-room. He disliked being questioned, even over trivial matters, and the way in which Mrs Mallin sometimes regarded him made him feel more of an outcast than the patient did himself.

Jim left the building and helped the doctor to put his pair of greys into the shafts. Jim's breakfast had done him good. He tried to show a lighthearted and jocular mood.

'All right, so you've got a lot of calls ahead of you. Aren't you goin' to ask me to ride along with you?'

Mallin clambered up to the box and kicked off the brake with one of his booted splayed feet. He gave Jim a clinical stare. 'Are you thinkin', perhaps, that you'd like to be away from the patient?'

Jim coloured suddenly and stuck his fists on his hips. 'Now look here, Dick, you surely don't think I'm likely to beat some sort of a confession out of Charlie, the state he's in an' all?'

Mallin clicked his tongue, and carefully adjusted his brown derby. He appeared to be taking his time in making up his mind about the question.

'You'll allow Charlie is a whole lot calmer than you are at this moment, Jim, but I don't think you're likely to commit any more offences against his person in the near future. In fact, you've been conductin' yourself rather well in the last twenty-four hours. Why don't you saddle up that horse of yours and ride along behind me? You know the direction I'll be takin' an' we could talk between visits, if you like.'

There was something which Mallin had to communicate. Jim knew this and he wondered what it was. He was beginning to get the feeling that this medical friend of his was a whole lot shrewder about certain things than he was himself. What in tarnation could the sawbones have found out concerning the Bayles' affairs by just attending to his patients?'

'All right, you can roll. I'll take your suggestion an' catch up with you in five minutes. Don't hang back!'

Glad of the chance of a bit of movement, Jim blanketed and saddled his big grey stallion and stood back while it arched its neck at him and twitched its coal-black tail. He gave its mane a few gentle tugs, adjusted his spurs and hoisted himself up into the saddle.

In spite of his haste, nearly ten minutes had elapsed before the horse and rider overtook the buckboard with its paired team. Jim moved in alongside and leapt to the box, still holding the reins. He attached the disappointed grey to the tailboard and moved a little nearer to his friend who appeared to have assumed the role of his conscience.

'There was something you wanted to communicate to me, Dick. That much was clear. So why not out with it this minute?'

There were times when Mallin did not appear to hear exactly what was said to him. After a lapse of a minute, during which the wheels on Jim's side squealed over some small loose stones, the doctor sighed.

'Before I say what I have to say, tell me a little about your brother. I remember you told me your folks both died in an epidemic, so I support you must have had a lot to do with raisin' him.'

Without acquiring any temporary lines, Jim's thoughtful face appeared to age for a minute or two. 'Yes, that was how it was. The folks, our mother and father, both died within a few hours of each other. It was not long after the war. As you know, my brother, Heck, was too young to be in the fighting.

'I tried to get him a little more schoolin', but that didn't work out too well, and some of the jobs I lined up for him did not hold him for very long. Then we parted for a while. Some of our family friends thought I was ridin' him too hard, tryin' as I was to be both a father an' a mother to him.'

Jim sighed hard and stared forward, as though examining the trail ahead through the bobbing ears of one of the horses.

'Did he get into trouble?' Dick prompted gently.

'Yes, he did,' Jim admitted. 'Then I ran him out of the county an' over the territorial line into New Mexico. I made him work with me then, on a ranch and with a freightin' line. A man I had met in the army gave him a temporary job as a constable in a new town. He didn't like that much, but he did a lot of practisin' with a revolver to pass the time. His real opportunity came when a veteran federal officer came through the town at a time when Heck was doin' rather well in a shootin' contest.

'This marshal, a former army colonel, liked the look of him an' took him on his staff. At that time or thereabouts, I parted from Heck an' left his future in more capable hands. His trainin' with the federal people apparently suited him, because he began to slowly build a reputation for himself as a trouble-shooter on difficult cases which overstepped the territorial lines.'

Jim paused for breath, and the doctor went on.

'And so he came into this part of Texas and gradually got himself involved with the outlaws who were terrorisin' the countryside. I know how you must feel about him, Jim. I jest wanted to hear you talk about him. If I can do anything to clarify your thoughts over this Garnett business, I might do you a bit of good.'

Jim nodded and looked away. 'But you didn't bring me along here jest to talk about my brother.'

'No, I didn't, Jim. And that's the truth. Since you came back into my life I've been very interested in your affairs. I came across an old newspaper the other day, one which talked about the Garnett era in all its aspects. You talked about their havin' gone to earth, and about your brother bein' missin' from that time forward. But there was something else which you never mentioned.'

Jim was clearly startled. He had an

idea what Dick was getting at, but he waited for him to explain.

'The loot which the Garnetts were supposed to have taken, Jim. The Western Settlers Association funds, old friend. Stolen from a bank which had only been operatin' for a little over a year. The loot has been missin' ever since, as well as the personalities we know about. How come you've never mentioned the loot?'

Jim felt like losing his temper, but he declined on this occasion and made Dick wait for his reaction. He yawned.

'Are you supposin' I'm doin' all this, shootin' Charlie an' such, because I want the Settlers Association funds?'

'Folks sometimes want things subconsciously, Jim, without ever actively thinkin' about them. Do you aim to find out about the loot at the same time as you locate your brother?'

'If one leads me to the other, yes, Dick. Otherwise, the loot doesn't draw me. I'm surprised you lured me all this way jest to find out if I was on the trail of a fortune. I am really. And right now, I figure I'll cut loose an' ride that restless grey in back of us.'

Jim did as he had intimated. The doctor thoughtfully watched him swing away. Before the distance between them made communication impossible, Mallin called: 'I'm only tryin' to help you understand yourself!'

Jim gave him an empty laugh and turned back along the track.

★ ★ ★

The revolver shots, though muted by distance, echoed across the local terrain to the north of town and had the effect of putting Jim in a panic. All he could think of was that Charlie had had a sudden recovery and that he was shooting everyone in sight through sheer joy, or frustration. He gave the grey a touch of the rowel. For a time, as the doctor's isolated home drew nearer, he wondered if he was altogether wrong in his surmising about the shots.

The narrowing distance, however, and the reactions of a lonely prospector going further north, went a long way to confirming that the shooting was at the Mallins' place.

Jim's imagination worked overtime. The first flurry had been about five or six shots. Then there was an interval. Next came another cylinder full at short fixed intervals. What if Charlie were tormenting Mrs Mallin, killing her slowly or making her think she was near to death?

Jim had a glimpse of Dick Mallin's face in his mind's eye. He felt that if Charlie really had gone berserk Dick would at last lose his temper and his detached view of life and blame everything that had happened upon him, Jim Bayles. The unwanted friend from the past.

The stallion was going flat out when Jim raced it over the final furlong and started to loosen his Colt from the holster at his right hip. After a brief interval, the shooting broke out again;

slow, careful shooting with a definite plan to it.

At first it sounded as if it was in the house, and then it occurred to Jim that it was beyond, in a semi-scrub garden where Mallin sometimes grazed his horses. Mabel Mallin stepped out of the house and came to the edge of the gallery, waving a drying cloth at him and actually smiling as though she was pleased to see him back again.

Jim hauled the grey to a spectacular stop and then walked it towards her. 'Mrs Mallin? Is there any sort of trouble here?'

'Shucks, Jim, there's a whole lot of noise that is particularly tryin' to the ears after a while. But nothin' more than that. The fact is, Charlie has redis-covered his talent for quick-fire revolver shootin'. He's bangin' away at bottles an' tin cans for all he's worth, an' that boy sure is a mighty fine marksman!'

Jim's doubts and misgivings showed in his face. Mabel led him into the house and through to the kitchen where it was possible to watch the marksman at work unnoticed. Charlie was bareheaded, apart from his substantial bandage, and every time he fired — first with one hand and then with the other — a beatific smile replaced his frown of concentration.

'Leave him be, Jim,' Mrs Mallin suggested. 'He's recoverin' a little an' that's what we all want for him. Ain't it?'

Jim nodded numbly, toying with his tight-banded stetson and mussing up his flattened jet-black hair.

'I had a talk with him before he went out there. He knows you're a travellin' man, an' he wants to move around with you, as your bodyguard. Now ain't that something?'

Jim nodded and sat down in a tall wicker chair.

'I think you're measurin' your patience, Jim, an' a whole lot of other things. Like maybe someone might want to take Charlie away from you an' slap him in jail before he's answered the questions which trouble you. I think you're worryin' too much. He has confidence in you. My husband doesn't want him jailed. We could alter his appearance if it would help. Take off that rather noticeable thin black beard and moustache. Maybe get a different sort of replacement for that shabby black hat that won't fit on account of the head bandage.'

'We could get him a whole new rigout that would jest about transform him. No one but his close relations would be able to pick him out in ordinary circumstances.'

Jim had added his suggestions in a quiet voice. It was difficult to detect enthusiasm. He was realising all over again the enormity of the task which he had set himself in binding Charlie Garnett to him in this unorthodox and somewhat unexpected way.

★ ★ ★

Charlie made himself agreeable to all three of the people who shared the house with him. He agreed to have his beard and moustache removed, to be clad in an entirely different outfit, and even to wear a tall undented fawn stetson.

During the last evening the two visitors were to spend under the Mallins' roof, Charlie surveyed himself in the long mirror screwed to a wall of the hall. The other three clustered behind him, awaiting his reaction. At last he smiled.

'I think you're tryin' to hide me for some good reason,' he remarked easily. 'Still, that's likely for the best. I can't be a good bodyguard to a writing gent if I keep drawin' trouble to myself. I figure I'm right in thinkin' my last image wouldn't do either of us a lot of good for the future.'

Neither of the watching men deigned to comment. Mabel Mallin drew Charlie into the kitchen on the pretext of making some slight adjustment to the band of the new stetson to further accommodate the light bandage still protecting his temple.

4

Towards the end of that week, Jim and Charlie were a good day's ride away from Blackrock in a south-easterly direction. Unknown to the latter, they were still prowling the terrain into which the Garnetts and the following posses had ridden during those fateful few days two years earlier.

When they first left the comparative security of the doctor's house, Jim had felt a sudden mounting of tension. As he laid himself down to rest, at nights, for instance, he kept wondering if Charlie would experience a sudden revelation as to what had occurred in the ghost town. If that happened, would the young outlaw revert to type and simply blast him without warning?

Time and the pleasant atmosphere out of doors between towns gradually healed Jim's somewhat raw nerves and went a long way towards developing a kind of working partnership between the two men who had elected to stay together on trail.

Jim had taken the opportunity of preparing quite a quantity of article work while he stayed with his doctor friend. This had been unloaded upon the local newspaper proprietor or telegraphed to other towns in southern Texas. He was well up to date with his commitments, which he thought wise in the existing circumstances.

During a midday break for coffee and rest, Jim thought the time was ripe to spring a surprise on Charlie. He fished out of his pocket an old photograph, worn at the corners. It showed Hector Bayles, his brother, some two and a half years earlier, in a head-and-shoulders portrait, sporting his federal deputy's badge and a broad, confident smile.

'Who do you think this is, Charlie?' Jim enquired.

He was stretched out on his back, resting his weight on an elbow.

51

Charlie's calm expression suddenly changed, as though he was haunted by the need to remember things long forgotten. He hunched his rounded shoulders and rubbed a thumb and forefinger along his backward-curving nose.

'You never stop tryin', do you, Jim?' he complained, long before he actually saw the photo.

With a sigh, he took the proffered pasteboard and gave a long look at it. It was at once clear that Hector Bayles' features meant nothing to him, but he did dwell upon the likeness out of sheer curiosity.

Jim examined the end of his small cigar. A little of the old tension was back.

'I don't know the fellow at all, amigo,' Charlie intimated quietly. 'Are you very disappointed? Does he mean an awful lot to you? Are you, by any chance, a peace officer like this grinnin' fellow wearin' the badge?'

Jim received the photo back again.

'No, I'm not a peace officer, Charlie. This is a picture of a man who disappeared some little time ago. You aren't the first person I've asked about him. I'm sorry if I seem to be gettin' at you all the time.'

'Looks like a fellow in his middle twenties. Hair? Brown, I'd say. He seemed to have plenty of it in the sideburns. Tallish, deep chested? How does that seem to you?'

'You're a good guesser, Charlie, but you still don't remember ever havin' seen him, so let's talk of other things, huh?'

Charlie sniffed. He removed his tall undented stetson with a care to which he had become accustomed, discarded the butt of a brown paper cigarette and turned abruptly to Jim. 'I've got a subject. My name. Seein' as how you went to great trouble to alter my appearance, I figure you wouldn't want me to use my old name, even if you knew it. So what are we goin' to call me? I raise the question now, on account of that hombre we met this mornin'. The one who was goin' to the town celebration in Placer City. I'd like for *us* to go there, seein' as how a writing gent of your calibre can do his work anywhere he likes. So . . . give me a name?'

Jim had already given time to this problem, which he knew was bound to crop up. 'Why don't we jest call you Charlie Crease, for the time bein'? We can think of a more permanent surname at a later date. What do you think?'

Charlie's features became inscrutable. His restless brown eyes narrowed to slits. Jim felt troubled again. But this time there was no serious cause for anxiety. Suddenly Charlie beamed. He raised a hand to the light bandage ringing his head.

'On account of this crease in the head that someone gave me, huh? That ain't a bad sort of name at all for a fellow who's lost part of his faculties, is it now?'

Jim agreed, but he did not enthuse.

At three o'clock the following afternoon, the tall retired lawyer in the silk hat who was controlling the special pistol shooting contest in Main Street, Placer City, clambered up on his box in the square and directed his hoarse voice through a megaphone at the crowd, which had dwindled a little due to the afternoon heat.

'Ladies and gentlemen, our contest, which started this morning with fifteen marksmen from all over the United States, has now dwindled to four. The four men left in are as follows: Skinner Johnson from Utah; Charlie Crease, who believes he belongs to Texas; Vance Smith, from Arizona; an' Willie Brough from right here in this little old town.'

The announcer paused while a ragged cheer and some hand-clapping occurred. He then asked the spectators to back off a bit at the other end of the square and showed the men entrusted to the throwing up of small metal discs

55

to those who took the contest seriously.

The marksmen shot in the order in which they were named. Jim Bayles found it hard to keep himself at the front of the crowd on account of those who surged out of the saloons and pushed in from the rear. He did, however, manage to stay within sighting distance of what was going on.

At first, Jim had been very vigilant about Charlie. He had wondered if this sort of action, pistol-shooting, might bring out into the open someone who had known the outlaw in the past. Perhaps Matt Garnett, or one of his spies. No one had shown any special interest in the small man in the tall hat, and gradually Jim's interest had changed to that of an involved spectator.

Skinner Johnson pulled his guns and did his snap-shooting first. Altogether, he was asked to shoot at twelve discs. The crowd grew excited as the giant moustached former buffalo-hunter winged the first ten discs without apparent effort. There was a brief pause before the last two went up, and as they were close together, Skinner took it rather easy. To his surprise, and the surprise of others watching, he missed one, and finished with a score of eleven out of twelve.

After another brief round of ballyhoo, Charlie stepped forward. He appeared as if he was uncomfortable in his big hat. He moved it this way and that to get the maximum amount of eye protection from the sun without masking his vision. At last, he pronounced himself ready, and he stood in a half-crouch with a weapon in each hand, scanning the sky with his restless brown eyes.

All went well with the first six shots. Somehow, the marksman missed the seventh. His concentration appeared to waver, but at the critical moment, as the eighth disc went up, Jim said quietly: 'You're doin' all right, amigo!'

His voice must have carried and Charlie's confidence was restored. He finished off in fine style, looking as if he could have winged ten more without undue strain, and the crowd gave him unrestrained praise for the way in which he had shot. He, too, had scored eleven.

Jim welcomed him out of the crowd while his results were being called out. Side by side and fully relaxed, they watched the other two men, Vance Smith and Willie Brough, go through their efforts. The local partisan crowd seemed pleased when the man from Arizona achieved only three hits and more or less finished off his chances for any further advancement.

Willie Brough was a young man in his thirties, the son of a local publican. Obviously, he could shoot well, but something in his complexion suggested to the visitors that he might have been imbibing a strong pick-me-up to settle his nerves. He started well enough, bowing to the crowd and doffing his hat. He winged the first four discs with a long-barrelled revolver and then burped.

The discs continued to fly, but his aim was off. He missed four of the last six and ended up with six hits out of twelve, and quietly blaming the state of his gun. One or two regular drinkers in his father's saloon took him by the shoulders and went through the nearest batwings.

The contest controller called for a half-hour's rest before the final between Charlie Crease and Skinner Johnson.

★ ★ ★

The two riding partners drank a couple of beers in the rest period. Charlie appeared to tense up a little in spasms. Consequently, Jim tried to distract him by making comments on others.

'Imagine a buffalo-skinner bein' as good with a hand gun as that Skinner Johnson from Utah. I would have thought that a slow-movin' animal like a buffalo would have been the easiest target goin' an' more for a man with a rifle.'

Charlie shook his head. 'You never can tell what a man does in his spare time. Especially if his hobby is fire-arms.'

As soon as he had spoken, Charlie raised his sparse brows and looked Jim straight in the face. 'I suppose for a man who can't remember anything, I said quite a mouthful jest then?'

'You surely did, amigo,' Jim acknowledged.

He glanced away, not wanting Charlie to tense up at that critical time. Charlie tried not to. He glanced down at his worn easy-draw holsters and studied the smoothness of them. He then removed his hat and made sure that his freshly-healed temple scar was not sticking to the band. He was looking away when he said what he had in mind.

'Do you think I'll ever remember, Jim?'

For the first time, he sounded a little pathetic. Jim had to cast around in his thoughts for something to give him the necessary boost for the rest of the contest.

'I think you will, Charlie. After all, you haven't been out of touch for very long. Besides, that cayuse of yours still knows you. The pinto acts like you've been together all your ridin' days, an' that's for sure.'

Charlie's eyes widened with interest. Even in the semi-gloom of the saloon where dust motes swam in the slanting rays of the sun, it was clear that confidence and vigour were back in the troubled marksman. His irises were a bright chocolate brown.

'I don't know why that should make me feel good, pardner, but it has. You know, with a bit of luck I could win this contest. What are they offerin'? One hundred dollars?'

Jim confirmed the nature of the prize, and as a man came along the street shaking a hand-bell he conducted Charlie out of doors.

★ ★ ★

61

The contest organisers had something special for the final shoot-out. The first part of it consisted of a line of green bottles, spaced out at one-foot intervals along a wooden bench three feet above the ground. This was for accuracy. Skinner shot first and scored the maximum, and the excitement touched a new high when Charlie stepped out in front of the others and achieved the same score.

Then came the last big test. At the other end of the square, at the maximum distance, the organisers brought in a special contraption invented by a retired carpenter who lived in the town. It consisted of a long bench with sets of handles at either end. Bars were connected to the handles of which there were two at each end. As a handle was turned, so a number of flat silhouettes, shaped out of metal to look like bottles, rose into view on the bench top.

There were four variations. There could be six, or seven, or thirteen or fourteen standing at the same time.

Those working the handles could lower the targets again as they saw fit. The main difficulty from the point of view of the marksmen was not knowing where the targets would pop up next. Even though there might be fourteen on the one bar, they were not all together.

The inventor sided the chief organiser and much was made of the contraption before everyone was satisfied, and Skinner Johnson, who had not seen anything like it before, stepped forward swinging his weapons by the trigger guards.

Much store was set by the timing of this event. Two notables stood adjacent to the target bench, checking one another with big flat watches. No one spoke as the shooting began. Up came six silhouettes and Skinner banged away with both guns, twitching his splendid moustache as he did so.

The handles were manipulated every ten seconds and by the time a minute had gone the man from Utah had scored twenty-seven using six guns.

Johnson seemed moderately pleased, although he was still a little baffled by the new style of target. He knew that he had done reasonably well, but now, when it was too late to make changes, he found himself wishing that he had shot last instead of first.

Charlie seemed reluctant to leave Jim's side. 'You got any special ideas about the way I should treat these unusual targets, pardner?'

'You're the expert, Charlie. You have the right sort of guns an' the ability. Jest do it the way that seems right, huh? I'm sure you'll do as well as Skinner 'cause he seemed to be bothered about the swingin' handles in the first half-minute.'

The man with the megaphone called for Charlie again. Jim pushed him forward and the judges checked his guns. He moved out into the space where Skinner had operated and did a couple of practice draws to ease his nerves. His restless eyes strayed to Jim.

'Easy, boy,' the journalist called.

'Don't tense up!'

Charlie took a couple of deep breaths, nodded to the starter to show that he was ready, and gave his full attention to the bench at the other end. A slight creak and thirteen silhouettes swung into view. The small man banged away at them, doing well at first, as Skinner had done, while he was firing his own weapons.

As soon as they were empty, he dropped on his right knee, grabbing for two of the spare guns laid in a line by his feet. He stayed on one knee and banged off several accurate shots before half-rising and going down on the other knee. Again, he blasted away with the knee touching the ground and his score mounted very steadily.

Somehow, he seemed to sense when the targets were going to be changed, and he kept up his firing from the knee level like a dancer doing an alternate knee routine.

A hoarse voice called, 'Time!' and a small man dropped the handle for the last time. Charlie went down on both knees and dropped his smoking guns, lacing his fingers and cracking his knuckles as the tension broke over him.

Jim was fascinated by the knee routine of shooting. Clearly it was something which Charlie had done before, and something which he had done well. But had he done it by way of an entertainment, or had he used his unique stance to blast his enemies?

The old man with the megaphone lurched up on to his box. 'Ladies and gentlemen, the winner, who has a score of thirty-six, is Charlie Crease!'

A great roar of acclaim went up, while Charlie moved around the cleared area, nodding and smiling and doffing his big hat to those who now treated him like a hero. The organiser tried to get silence, but failed. His voice also went back upon him.

He was explaining that the presentation would take place in the Last Chance Hotel when a man with a much more powerful voice began to make his presence felt on the other side of the crowd.

'I tell you I've come across that knee-level shootin' routine before today. It was in a rodeo somewhere. A fellow shot like that an' some of the folks said he had a name that was the same as some outlaw! Can't think what it was right now, but the name will come back to me!'

Another person with a higher pitched voice answered, 'If he's ever been an outlaw, I'd gamble he's seen a few human targets at the other end of those guns!'

Jim heard the words, along with many others. Charlie appeared to be looking to Jim for guidance. At the same time, the man with the booming voice called again. He was trying to get into direct touch with Charlie, who seemed a bit doubtful about the development.

Jim heightened himself on tiptoe and beckoned Charlie out of the crowd. He came quickly enough and was helped through the fringe of bodies. Jim whispered for him to take off his hat, and after that it was easy to get away from the searching crowd who wanted to be close to him.

5

At the foot of the steps which led up to the foyer of the Bonanza Hotel, Charlie Crease paused and turned to face his partner.

'Jim, oughtn't we to be goin' directly to the Last Chance to collect my winnings?'

Ignoring the question, Jim asked in his turn, 'That man who shouted in the crowd. The one who wanted to get into touch with you on account of your knee sharp-shootin', did his voice sound familiar to you?'

'No, it didn't. The only thing which seemed familiar was shootin' off one knee and then the other. That stance gave me the confidence to win the first prize. I did good, didn't I?'

Jim blinked and nodded. Any moment he felt that someone might come along the street and ask why the winner of the contest was not in the right place to collect his winnings.

'I shan't remember him, Jim. Can't we go along there now? You'll side me while I collect the prize, won't you?'

Jim sank down into a sitting position on the lowest step. 'Charlie, there's a chance that man with the loud mouth might bring back your memory with a jerk. It might be good an' painful for you, if it happened in the middle of hundreds of people. Will you trust me, give the Last Chance a miss? I'll see you get your hundred dollars, jest the same!'

Charlie was baffled for once. His expression showed that he was really beyond comprehension of his unique situation in life. Clearly, he wanted to trust Jim, but his pride was willing him otherwise. In the distance, down the street, men were shouting as though impatient for his presence. At length, he sighed, glanced up the steps and nodded.

'Okay, then, jest so long as I get my

winnings, one way or the other. Let's go.'

The short-sighted male receptionist seemed surprised when they approached his desk at a time when all the rest of the town seemed to be occupied elsewhere.

'Something I can do for you, sir?'

'Billy McDoogle, the owner of the *Placer Pioneer*, was supposed to book a double room in the name of Jim Bayles. Did he do that?'

'Why, sure, Mr Bayles. Your room is number four, on the upper floor. Are you wantin' to go up there right now?'

'My friend has a slight headache. He wants to lie down. Myself, I'm goin' lookin' for Mr McDoogle. You don't happen to know if he'll be in his office?'

The clerk went off into a rapid series of blinks. 'Well now, he's mighty keen on the pistol shootin' but at the same time he's short of assistants. I'd say you stand a fifty-fifty chance of locatin' him in his office, Mr — er — Bayles.'

Jim nodded and smiled. He signed in

rapidly, handed the key over to Charlie who mounted the stairs with a slight look of disbelief in his eyes. As soon as Charlie was out of sight, Jim walked hurriedly out of the hotel and began to cross town in the direction of the newspaper office.

He found it without difficulty, but the owner and editor was not there. Billy McDoogle had left a note pinned to the door saying he would be back in a half-hour. Jim entered the diminutive office which smelled of ink and news-print and flopped into the swivel chair which seemed over big when the owner was in it. He found himself swinging a leg and thinking over the latest development. Why had he pulled Charlie out of the limelight?

Had he actually done it to prevent the young outlaw painful memories? Had *he*, Jim Bayles, gone that soft in the head? Or had he whisked Charlie away in case that fellow with the loud mouth convinced everybody that Charlie was kin to outlaws? If the real reason was the latter, then it meant that Jim had been afraid to lose his only contact with the gang before he acquired his vital information.

McDoogle's short booted steps were sounding on the boards outside while Jim contemplated. At last, the young journalist put aside his self-examination. He was still not sure whether he had acted to protect Charlie or his own interests.

The little newspaper owner came in muttering imprecations. He fixed Jim with a stony stare and pointed an inky forefinger at him.

'You, Jim Bayles, are no sort of a lucky omen to me. My assistant has a fever. I have a newspaper to get out. I take a few minutes off to see the presentation of a prize, an' what do you know? The winner disappears! He doesn't even appear to collect his hundred dollars! I give up. Let me have my chair.'

Jim grinned, tossed his hat on to the hat stand, and stood up.

'You don't have to give up, old timer. The winner is my friend. Right now, the winner is in the room you booked for me, takin' it easy. The fact is, he's had trouble due to a bullet wound. That reception planned for him might not do him any good at all. Trust me, I know. I want you to go back to the Last Chance before they decide to give the prize to Skinner Johnson and bring it back here.'

'It'd have to be in the next hour, but — '

'Bring it back here on behalf of the winner, and I'll be writing out for you an exclusive article on a subject which is always good for circulation. The Garnett family of outlaws. In particular I shall be writing about a young man named Charlie Garnett. I shall want you to print my article in full, after I've left town. Now, how about gettin' back to that reception hall for the prize money?'

McDoogle had removed his tall hat and shiny frock-coat. In the depths of his chair, he regarded the pensive young man in front of him, his metal-rimmed spectacles perched high on his wrinkled forehead and the short, spiky white hair on his crown sticking up even higher.

'It would have to be accompanied by a photo of the author, I think,' the small man bargained calmly.

'I agree. So now get along and collect that hundred dollars. The name of my friend is Charlie Crease, mind you don't get it wrong in case the old lawyer doesn't want to pay out. I'll get you your hat.'

'And furthermore,' the little man resumed, 'I must have the right to make my own comment upon the contents of the article and the man who wrote it.'

'I'll agree to that, as well, provided me an' my charge have already left town.'

Jim propelled Mr McDoogle as far as the door, informing him that there was no further news of the missing deputy federal marshal, Hector Bayles. Left on his own, he resumed his seat in the editor's chair and pulled from the side pocket of his dark jacket the pad on which he usually wrote out his articles.

He wrote down a few essential details from memory and then started to think a little more deeply. He knew the location of McDoogle's newspaper museum where he kept old copies of the *Pioneer* and he made a short visit to the room where they were kept.

Several copies dated approximately a couple of years earlier provided great interest. He brought them back with him to the big scarred desk in the editorial room and perused them one by one. Nothing in them was new to him. In fact, a lot of the material had been written by himself.

Some forty minutes later, he pushed the old yellowing papers aside and asked himself what was the basic aim behind this article he was going to write. He wanted to draw Matt Garnett out into the open. The chances were that Charlie would not remember anything helpful for some time to come.

But Charlie belonged to the Garnetts, even if he was not as close as the brothers.

If they knew he was consorting with Jim Bayles, brother of the federal officer who had hounded them almost into the ground two years earlier, maybe they would make some sort of a positive move. If they showed themselves, then Jim could further his compulsive ambition to know the truth.

He started to write with painstaking slowness, going back over his loops because the pencil was not as sharp as he would have liked. In his early paragraphs he refreshed the memories of the *Pioneer*'s readers by giving a résumé of the gang's activities, listing bank raids, strikes against isolated hamlets, road agent work against stage-coaches and freight wagons. He added the known number of killings which were believed to have been committed by them. It was into double figures.

Having established the background,

he then began on the new material, the speculation as to what might happen if Matt Garnett, his brothers and other associates could be proved to be back in south-western Texas for the purpose of linking up again to organise crime.

What had they returned for if, in the past, the activities of lawmen such as Heck Bayles had driven them into obscurity? Had they come back to molest the people of this developing country, or had they come back to recover something which had been lost to them before, when they dropped out of circulation?

And then, just to stir up the interest to a higher level, Jim built into the article a further bit of speculation. How would it be, he asked the reader, if one of the gang — say, young Charlie Garnett — had cut himself off from the others and was running about with someone who had definitely no reason to feel any sympathy with them? What might happen then?

As soon as he had finished it, Jim

knew that he had struck the right sort of note. He polished up his phraseology here and there and read it over a couple of times before relaxing.

He found himself speculating as to what Matt and the others had been doing since their small setback in the ghost town. They would not be advertising their presence unnecessarily. Not after their experiences of the other year. Surely, their actions would depend upon whether they thought Charlie was dead or alive?

If this far they had assumed him to be dead, then the newspaper article would tell them that they were wrong. After this, if they wanted to free him, or to get him away from anyone they considered undesirable, they would indulge in concerted action. After all, they had pride like everyone else, and the man who had held them up in Ghost Town Creek had taken liberties with them.

They would come, sooner or later. That conspicuous pinto horse which was so attached to Charlie would give them a valuable clue. What if they already knew it was housed in a certain big livery in this town? They could be waiting for its owner to collect it, along with his new riding partner!

Jim stood up and shrugged his shoulders, as though he were trying to shrug away unpleasant thoughts. He sat down again, and dozed in the chair, not awakening until he heard the newspaper owner chuckling over his article.

For a man so small in stature, McDoogle had a rather deep fruity laugh. He added a few extra chuckles when he noticed the startled look on the awakening man's face.

6

The joint occupants of room four on the upper floor of the Bonanza Hotel had packed their gear, eaten their breakfast and were in a position to leave town by half past eight, but they still had one call to make which Jim insisted was important.

The town photographer's small establishment was near the end of Third Street where the property was cheap to rent. He shared a double shop with a maker of leather articles and seemed very effusive when he opened the door for them.

'You want I should stay with the horses, Jim, or should I come inside?' Charlie asked quietly.

'Please yourself, amigo. This won't take long.'

Charlie nodded. The sun was not yet very hot, and there was plenty of shade in the street. He elected to remain under the sidewalk awning until Jim was ready. People went by, men and women. Some were old and some were young. Some looked friendly, and others anything but friendly. There were pompous people; folks who had achieved a lot in life and who walked in such a way that no one was in a hurry to pass the time of day with them.

Youngsters in good suits paraded past. Other children dressed in old cast-offs and hand-me-downs. They all looked a little different and none of them acted exactly alike. There was a leavening of Mexicans and one or two negroes, as well.

After a time, Charlie tired of watching them. He leaned back on the bench, stuck his thumbs in his belt and gave himself over to conjecture. What manner of man was he really? Did he have a woman waiting for him somewhere? A wife, perhaps, who knew that he was overdue and who did not know why? What if he were the father of children? And where might they be, these imaginary relations of his? Near Ghost Town Creek? It was highly unlikely that they would live in Blackrock where Dr Mallin operated, or Placer City, where they were now.

Where then? If he didn't have them with him when the shooting incident took place in the ghost town, then he must have been looking for something, or for some location. Perhaps doing a job between towns. Maybe they lived in the country. He could be a prospector, or the owner of a small isolated homestead! Other things occurred to him, but the possibilities were too many for easy conjecture.

Charlie sighed, yawned and closed his eyes. It was not yet time to exchange his present world for the one which he had known before; the one in which he had lived for nearly thirty years.

Where did they overlap, the old world and the new? Was there anything else to it, other than a chance meeting in a town long since abandoned by humans?

His mind slid away from the compulsive conjecturing and he dozed.

★ ★ ★

The photographer's studio was not particularly well lighted. Alfonso, the man who ran it, depended upon a flash to get the results he needed for his portraits. He was a plumpish man with Mexican blood who used the lavish compliments of the Latin tongue in the everyday vernacular of white Americans.

Jim, who was also in a thoughtful mood, tired of his constant flow of language and complained at the third pose, one in a standing position against a scenic backcloth.

'Mr Alfonso, all this is really unnecessary, I feel sure. The newspaper proprietor merely insisted on having a picture taken so that he could reproduce something to go alongside of my work! All he wanted was a head and shoulders! Where would he find the space for a full-length photo of me with a river and mountain background?'

Alfonso's hair was thick and luxuriant on the head and in his beard and moustache. It was nearly white, and that gave away a clear indication of his age. He protested with a flowing hand gesture.

'Forgive me, *Señor* Bayles, I get so few opportunities to exercise my talents on men who are truly handsome. With your permission I will just take this picture and then I am finished. By the way, who is paying the bill for my work?'

Jim lifted his straight brows. The expression in his blue eyes hardened. 'You mean to tell me that wasn't made clear when McDoogle made the appointment? *He* pays, of course! It was his idea in the first place!'

Alfonso nodded, gave a strained smile and retired behind his apparatus. Jim was still breathing hard when the flash flared for the last time and the sitting was over. He hastily shook hands with the photographer and hurried out into the street as if he could not breathe indoors.

The sight of Charlie, head back and dozing on the bench, had the effect of calming him down. He slowed in his tracks, walked slowly up the boards and sat down beside his riding partner. His weight on the bench had the effect of rousing the sleeper. They glanced at one another, exchanged nods and at once moved towards the horses.

*   *   *

Around eleven o'clock in the morning, the two riders started to come up with a low spine-backed ridge. As a vantage point it attracted Jim, who at once suggested that it might make a good spot for a short halt.

In a small hollow located in a break along the spine Charlie, in his usual jog-along fashion, built a low fire and set up the coffee pot to boil. This far, since Placer City, the conversation had been minimal. Now, judging by the give-away brightness of Charlie's eyes, that was to be remedied.

When the coffee was poured, Jim found it too hot to drink straight away. From where he was reclining he could see a long way on either side of the ridge and there were no humans in sight. Consequently, he was fairly relaxed.

'You look like a man who has things on his mind, amigo. Maybe now is a good time to air them,' he invited.

Charlie shifted his battered mug from one hand to the other, burning his fingers. 'Yesterday, Jim, was quite an eventful day. For the first time since we met I knew a little enjoyment. I'm referrin' to the pistol shootin' contest, of course. I had the impression when the competition was on that you enjoyed it as well.'

'I did enjoy it. I was pleased for you. So?'

Charlie shook his head as though not

comprehending. He grinned, but there was not a lot of mirth behind it. 'Well, so I get pulled away at the climax, before I can show myself at the hotel an' collect my winnings. And today, who should go along and have his photograph taken? Not the winner of the competition, but the winner's friend, for publication in the local paper. What can you say to that?'

Before Jim could say anything at all, Charlie resumed : 'An' while you were in the photographer's shop, I got to thinkin' about myself again. I think you know a whole lot more about me, about who I am, than you've ever tried to explain. Jim, for Pete's sake, do I have a wife? Do I have a family waitin' for me somewhere?

'If the answer is yes, then I ought to be told where to go to take up with my responsibilities again. Ain't that so? Will you answer me?'

Jim waved him into silence before he could get started again.

'I wouldn't want your photo in the

paper in case it did you more harm than good. That man at the shootin' contest. He was tryin' to put a name to you. He said you'd one time possibly worked in a rodeo, doin' that shootin' act off your knees, but he also said you had a name like a known and wanted outlaw.

'That's why I pulled you away without waitin' to know what he said. There are folks in these parts who are mighty keen to see anyone remotely connected with outlaws behind bars. I don't think it would be fair to give you over to a jailer when you can't properly remember things, an' that's a fact!

'As for me havin' my photo taken. That was a condition the little editor fellow insisted on. He went to collect for you, an' I wrote an article for him while he was away. He refused to co-operate with me unless I agreed to have my picture in the paper. I don't like photo publicity, but havin' my likeness in the paper might jest help us in our present situation.'

'An' what about the folks who might be expectin' me back? Do you know if I'm married, Jim?'

The dark-haired young man shook his head very decidedly. 'I don't have any means of knowing whether you are married or single, Charlie. For the present, I can't put your mind at rest on that point. All we can hope for is that if you have folks dependent upon you someone will look out for them.'

'Are you married, Jim?'

'No.'

'Then you couldn't really tell me what a married man feels like when he's away from his known haunts?'

Charlie's last question sounded critical and for once Jim was not enjoying the interrogation. 'I don't know what I haven't experienced, Charlie, an' that's a fact. I do know what it is like to be separated from my nearest kin an' not to know whether that person is alive or dead, though, an' I can tell you such a feelin' ain't pleasant. I've known what it felt like for over two years now, an' I still haven't learned to live with the uncertainty.'

There was so much conviction and depth in Jim's voice as he answered at length that Charlie stopped asking questions and automatically filled up both their coffee cups. Their eye glances above the cups suggested a truce.

★   ★   ★

Another hour of steady riding, this time towards the south, worked much of the ill-feeling out of the partners and healed the recent breach, brought about by uncertainty. Charlie had behaved well in that short time, giving a lot of attention to the broken ground over which they were travelling, and occasionally using his spyglass to check the different types of terrain.

Jim felt around for his small stock of stogie cigars. In doing so, he encountered a long slim envelope in his inside pocket. He blinked hard, realising that he had been so taken up with his inner troubling thoughts that he had not handed over Charlie's winnings.

'Charlie, come over here, will you?'

The shorter man was slow to lower his spyglass. When he condescended to do so, he turned and took a long look over his shoulder as though trying to weigh up what mood Jim was in. Jim grinned, and the stiffness went out of Charlie, who then turned his pinto and came back to talk in greater intimacy.

'Here's your winnings, Mr Crease.'

Charlie became bashful, and Jim beamed, wondering just how self-conscious he might have been had he been forced to receive the hundred dollars in front of two or three hundred vociferous people.

'It's my pleasure to hand over one hundred dollars to the best marksman of the day. Yesterday, to be more exact. Congratulations. You deserved to win, and you gave the other gunmen a really fine lesson in how to do it well.'

Charlie took the sealed envelope and toyed with it, while Jim discovered and lit a stogie. The winner ripped open the flap of the envelope with his knife blade and found to his surprise that the envelope contained a small folded certificate of merit, outlining the occasion and the sort of shooting necessary to win the award. It was made out to one Charlie Crease, outright winner, and was signed by no less than three notables of the town.

The wad of dollar bills were all of the same denomination and clean enough to have come straight from the printers.

Charlie examined them delicately as though he had never had notes of that calibre in his hands before. He glanced up and grinned, and Jim grinned back at him.

'You're a man of substance now, amigo. You can pay your way with clean notes.'

'Ain't that right? If there's anybody hopin' to get in touch with me on account of the past, they don't have to take on a pauper, an' that's for sure.'

Charlie tried two or three places

before he finally stowed away his banknotes just as they were inside his shirt. The difficulty of the undulating, unbroken earth beneath their horses' hooves did not bother them for quite a time. Charlie's good fortune appeared to have boosted them both, lifting their minds above the unknown considerations which so often left them ill-at-ease.

The first remark which cut across the good mood came from Charlie, as they were beginning to think for the first time of a night camping ground.

'Jim, when does that newspaper come out with your photograph in it?'

'This afternoon, in Placer City. Folks in other places might not see it till tomorrow. You know how it is with stagecoaches an' mail.'

Charlie knew how it was. He also knew that the publication of Jim's work and the photograph might materially alter their short-lived partnership together. And that, with a memory which still would not function properly, would be a change for the worse.

7

It was no accident that the three Garnett brothers, Matt, Lee and Drag, happened to be encamped near a creek used by coachmen out of Placer City on the eastward side. They had used the spot before, and from time to time observations made at that point had served them well as they laid their plans.

Around mid-morning, the eastbound coach slowed near the creek, as usual, so that the sweating team of six horses could be cast loose and taken down to the water's edge for a long drink before resuming their journey towards the county boundary, which happened to be the Pecos river.

On this particular day, the one after the publication of the *Placer Pioneer*, no less than three women and four men shared the interior of the coach for the journey east. The morning was hot and the coach, even with the help of its leather straps, was a rather uncomfortable mode of travel.

The driver and guard went off with the six horses. The older of the gentlemen travellers helped the ladies out of the coach, and for a period of nearly ten minutes the conveyance was left entirely unattended.

During the first of those minutes, the brother widely known as Drag (a nickname bestowed upon him by a trail crew) who was thirty-two years of age and the youngest of the trio, crawled out of some rather spiky scrub and crossed the few yards of eroded track to the coach, the nearside door of which was swinging open.

As soon as he was sure that no one could see him, Drag straightened up and casually peered in through the door. Whereas Matt's colouring of hair could be termed as auburn, and that of Lee as reddish, Drag's was definitely sandy. He rasped his thumb-nail around a fine crop of chin stubble reared in forty-eight hours. His fleshy mouth spread into a promising grin which revealed his yellow gapped teeth. His green eyes grew rounder as he noticed two small ladies' handbags made out of pretty coloured cloth lying on the seats.

Although he knew that the eyes of his dominating older brother, Matt, were fixed on him at a distance, Drag nevertheless took a chance by grabbing the two bags and checking over their contents. He was disappointed with both. They contained far less than he might have guessed. One of them he closed up again without misappropriating anything and the other conceded only a five-dollar bill.

The sort of item he was specially looking for lay on the far seat. He glanced around again, assured himself that the passengers were not yet returning, and then launched himself briefly into the interior after the newspaper which lay there fluttering like a fan.

Before he came out again he committed the five-dollar bill to the inner band of his hat. Five minutes later, he arrived back in the narrow dry ditch where the other two awaited him.

'How about that, then, brothers?' he remarked, feigning breathlessness. 'An Indian couldn't have done the job more skilfully. An' here's this week's newspaper, all laid out with news like we'd hoped!'

'Did you get the impression the passengers were rich enough to put the guns on them?' Lee queried, pulling at his ginger moustache.

'No, I didn't,' the younger man admitted. 'I — '

He was starting to explain, hoping not to give away the fact that he had explored the women's handbags against orders, when Matt snatched the paper out of his hands. Their eye glances met and Drag panicked and looked elsewhere.

'Brother, you're gettin' slow!' Matt complained.

He was about to say a whole lot more by way of criticism, but the sounds of men's raised voices and the clatter of horses' shoes cut across what they were doing. All three of them sank down into the narrow depression and brought up their rifles to a ready position.

Another three minutes elapsed before the passengers were all back in their seats and the crew and team were ready. Matt, as was usual with him, refused to allow his brothers to relax until the vehicle had travelled some fifty yards. Only then did he put aside the rifle and open out the newspaper.

His rapid, darting gaze went from one article to another, noting the gist of the headlines, but all the time seeking for something specific relating to themselves. He found it on one of the inside pages. His muted whistle almost parted his auburn wisp of a beard as he folded the sheets another way and pushed back his hat.

His younger brothers exchanged glances while he was busy, but they had the patience to wait for his revelations.

'For nearly two years I've been waitin' for everybody in these parts to forget the name of Garnett, and now some article-writin' hombre has undone all I've been strivin' for!'

'You mean we're actually mentioned right there in the paper?' Lee queried excitedly.

Matt nodded. He retained his hold upon the newspaper and shot a withering sidelong glance at the other two. 'Not only mentioned, in the headlines. We have a whole column more or less dedicated to us, followed up by the editor's comments on the article and the man who wrote it. And that ain't all! They've printed a picture of the journalist right alongside of it! Will you think of that?'

Neither of the younger pair could match Matt in reading, but rather than spell it all out to them when he wanted to think about the purport of the article, he surrendered the *Pioneer* to the other two and gave himself over to conjecture.

Ten minutes elapsed. During that time, Lee managed to get through the writing and handed over the appropriate part to Drag. The latter was slower, mouthing the words as he came to them and occasionally looking up to see if the other two were watching him.

Distantly, an impatient riding horse still wearing its slackened saddle, whinnied at the unparalleled delay. Matt began to whistle tunelessly to himself. It was a sign he was ready to discuss what they had just learned.

Drag put down the newspaper, his task not finished.

'What do you make of it, Matt?'

'That fellow whose picture is published is up to his neck in whatever's goin' on. That much is quite clear. He's supposed to be James H. Bayles, a travellin' journalist, with a special interest in our affairs.

'I think we know why he's interested in us. That — that federal marshal who hounded us over this wilderness to the south, almost to the Mexican border, he was called Bayles. This man and the other, who dropped out of circulation when we did, they're brothers!'

Although Lee had read everything, he had difficulty in reading behind the actual words. He frowned and asked for an explanation.

'An' do you think this James Bayles is takin' on where his brother left off? Is it jest that he wants us in jail, or danglin' from the end of a rope? Is that the sort of jasper we have to contend with?'

'It could be, but it's hard to say,' Matt confessed quietly. 'He's stirrin' things up. If he doesn't want us inside, then he wants to use us. He might be after us, an' that would mean his motive would be revenge or bounty. Otherwise, he wants the missin' loot, or simply information. But I can't think a fellow would go to all this trouble jest for information.'

Lee picked up the paper again and took another look at Jim Bayles' likeness. He bared his teeth. 'One thing,

Matt, we'll know this fellow when we meet up with him, an' we'll know what to do when the time comes around.'

'When we meet up with him again, you mean,' Matt corrected lightly.

'Are you suggestin' that Bayles was the fellow at the ghost town?' Drag asked unexpectedly.

The other two turned and stared at him. Both were surprised that he should have cottoned on to this notion as quickly as he did.

'That would be my guess, Drag,' Matt admitted. 'You see, that writer fellow jest doesn't know a good bit about us. He writes like he's obsessed with everything we've done in the past an' what we're likely to do now. And that ain't all. He's singled out for special comment cousin Charlie. Now there's a thing. I don't figure it's a coincidence. That man Bayles knows that Charlie has separated from us.

'He's tellin' us that Charlie is still alive and well. These are things he couldn't write about if he hadn't been at the ghost town that time. Charlie is a bit of a mystery. I can't quite figure why he might be keepin' Charlie right alongside of him. Or why Charlie would do it, either.

'I know he's not so close as the three of us here, but I never figured he'd take the opportunity to change sides! I mean, what could the man have said to him to set him against us for the future?'

Lee flicked the end of his moustache. 'You're forgettin' one thing, Matt,' he enthused.

'And what is that, brother?'

'If that article was aimed at the likes of us, every item in it doesn't have to be the truth, does it now? We've only got the written word tellin' us that Charlie's turned against us! So why couldn't Bayles be tellin' lies in print jest to upset us for the future?'

Matt was slow to unwind.

He began to talk again with a home-rolled cigarette in his mouth. 'Most men do things for money. If his brother ain't turned up again, how does that affect things? I don't know. If it's loot he wants, we can't help him. If it's bounty, we can deny him that by givin' him a rich dose of lead poisonin'. What do you say to that, brother Lee?'

'That's fightin' talk, Matt, an' we know fightin' better than most things. One other item puzzles me. How about them other fellows who are wantin' to join us? Malachi French, Rudy Hickstead an' Dan Bruce? If we're goin' to strike back at this Bayles fellow, shouldn't we get a bit more support?'

Matt chuckled and stared at Drag, but he did not react.

'Back there in the ghost town, Bayles was the one to ambush us. When we go against him, we pick the place and the time an' do the arrangin'. We should be able to cope with him all right. Those friends of ours can join us, but we'll let our trails cross naturally, huh?'

Lee nodded in agreement, but he did not know why Matt seemed reluctant to have the extra guns with him straight away. The leader, however, could read his thoughts.

'Three men movin' around like we are don't attract a lot of notice along the trails an' in the towns, but six men now, that's different. Six men movin' around together is a nice big round number. The kind of group that remains in somebody's memory. Right now, we want to pass unnoticed because we ain't rightly formulated any long-term plans. Do you see now, Lee?'

'I get you, Matt. So pretty soon we go lookin' for this Bayles hombre an' give him his deserts. That's right, ain't it? But where do we look? That's a problem, ain't it?'

Lee glanced up into the wide expanse of blue sky. Drag did the same. He always felt very much the underdog and he privately enjoyed the infrequent occasions when Lee presented Matt with a problem he could not solve right away. This time, however, he was to be disappointed. Matt had already thought out what he was going to say.

'Bayles must have been in Placer City recently, on account of that photograph. Now, if he's goin' over all the old territory we covered two years ago, his direction is bound to be south. What more do we need to know?

'In any case, we have to go that way to further our own ends, an' those three wanderin' guns you mentioned earlier are supposed to make their presence known nearer the border. So why don't we get on the move, an' keep lookin' as we ride? I have a feelin' that the immediate future is goin' to get busy an' stay that way, whether we three want it so or not. So let's go an' hit the leather.'

There was a scramble for the horses, which augured ill for their enemies.

8

Thirty minutes before nightfall a bird of prey, probably an eagle-hawk, swooped down out of a cloudless sky and snatched up a baby jackrabbit within fifty yards of where Charlie had built the night camp fire. He heard the beat of its wings, perceived the line of its dive and watched it withdraw with its prey. It was not until it was out of sight behind a tree copse that he realised he was gripping the butts of his guns with all his strength.

Jim came back out of the trees on the east side and perceived Charlie's frame of mind.

'It's goin' to be a full moon, amigo, but that doesn't mean we ought to be superstitious about it. How's that stew comin' along?'

'It smells real good, Jim, only I don't seem to have the appetite to do justice to it. Here, have a plateful. Me, I'll wait a while. I'll maybe eat mine while I'm keepin' guard tonight.'

'You think we'll need a guard, Charlie?' Jim probed.

'If we don't need a guard then all that business in the newspaper ain't goin' to do you a lot of good. Sure, we need a guard. In any case, ain't that what I'm here for? To act as your bodyguard? So eat up and don't let's talk about it any more. I guess that eagle I saw a few minutes ago rattled me. I wanted to blast off at it.'

Jim wondered why Charlie had restrained himself, but he declined to comment further. Within fifteen minutes the food was consumed and the coffee pot nearly empty. Jim lighted for himself a stogie and took a solitary walk around their camp.

They had located it in a slight depression of sandy soil mostly surrounded by light prickly scrub. There was no water to hand, but they had drunk their fill and tended the horses in a small pool of clear water an hour's ride away. To eastward, the ground was a little higher and clothed with timber of the dwarf pine variety. The two horses had been pegged out among the pines as a sort of safeguard should anyone try to get close from that direction.

Jim's nerves tingled a bit as he made the rounds, but he had no sort of hemmed-in feeling and although the light was fading fast there was nothing to suggest that they did not have that part of the county entirely to themselves. He yawned as he came back. Sufficient time had elapsed for the Garnetts to be in full possession of the news printed in the paper, and they could be on their way.

Somehow, Jim did not feel strongly about that. Perhaps it was the sight of Charlie squatting like a graven image just outside the range of firelight which made him feel secure. Charlie with a brace of revolvers and a useful dark-stocked shoulder weapon.

'Get into your blanket, why don't you?' Charlie prompted him.

'You don't want to talk then, pardner?'

'I don't want to talk, Jim, other than to say good night.'

'I'll call you in two hours, Charlie. I'll say my good night then, if it's all the same to you.'

Charlie chuckled but did not answer as Jim spread his long figure over the ground and patiently rolled himself in his thick two-colour blanket. The smart flat-topped dark stetson came off his head which was cautiously laid up against the soft leather of his saddle.

Lolling pensively against the stock of his rifle, Charlie studied Jim's silhouette in the gathering gloom. For a moment, the head resting against the hollow of the saddle made him think of a man about to be executed on a chopping block. He shuddered and wondered why such a macabre subject remained in his memory out of the scant knowledge of history which he possessed.

★ ★ ★

No clouds occurred to obscure the scudding moon, but the timber stand had the effect of hiding the moon glow from the camp site. Gradually, the kindling wood on the fire was consumed and sank low. Jim was soon asleep. His slow, measured breathing revealed that.

Charlie's head sank a little further forward, but otherwise he was as alert as ever. He had come along on this trip as a bodyguard, and he did not intend to be caught out on the first real challenge. After about an hour, his concentration was not quite so good. He had to work to keep up his self-imposed standard of alertness.

The effort cost him something. A blood vessel near the healed wound began to throb. He was brooding over the injury when the owl or owls hooted for the first time. At once, he came to full awareness, and his head swivelled slowly upon his neck.

He would have thought that there was not much hunting for owls to do in the prickly scrub. Surely such determined night campaigners would have done better in the trees in the other direction. Had he misjudged the direction of the night bird? No, the sound came again from almost the same place. A slight cold chill began to make itself felt along his spine.

★ ★ ★

In the owl area, Matt was forced to talk when he would have preferred to remain silent.

'Two owl hoots is enough. If that's Charlie over there somewheres he'll know the signal. It ain't as if we'd jest invented it, is it?'

Lee Garnett nodded and lowered his head. His hands were tightly gripping his shoulder weapon ready for the fusillade which would rip the night quiet to ribbons. Drag grunted and pulled away a foot or two on the other side. The latter had no sooner made this move than some slight movement took his eye.

Just beyond the halo created by the dying fire something or someone had moved. He rolled closer to Matt with sufficient momentum to put the older man in a state of nerves.

'What in tarnation are you up to, Drag? You got a burr in your shirt or something?'

'Nope, it ain't anything like that, Matt. I jest seen a movement. If you asked me to guess what caused it, I'd say a man was slippin' further away from the camp, maybe towards the trees!'

Matt made a slight noise indicating intense displeasure. Lee whispered a reason. 'What did you expect to see then? That was Charlie gettin' away from the line of fire, you fool! So keep quiet now till Matt gives the word!'

The still form in the bright blanket

was all that Matt was interested in. He cleared his throat noiselessly and wondered if there was any need for further delay. Suddenly, he thought he saw the sleeping man move. He tensed, but nothing further happened. He wondered how far Charlie had managed to crawl towards the trees.

★ ★ ★

Some sort of instinctive warning system deep down in his being made Jim shift a fraction and glance towards Charlie just about the same time when the others saw him move. The bodyguard had already travelled several yards, taking all his weapons with him, in a squirming newt-like motion when Jim perceived what was happening.

At first, the withdrawal was beyond Jim's comprehension. *Charlie withdrawing* . . . . There could be only one explanation for that, and he did not dare to think about it. There was likely to be some sort of premeditated attack and Charlie had received word of it. Unless he was preparing to do the dirty work himself!

Shattered as Jim was by the withdrawal of his partner, the man who had appeared to take so seriously this job of night bodyguard, he still could not believe that his man was about to throw down upon him himself.

But a withdrawal in the face of danger, without a warning. That was serious. In a matter of seconds, Jim could no longer tell the whereabouts of the withdrawing figure and he felt as though he was stark naked in the presence of all the outlaws at large in the territory.

He fought to control a kind of ague in his limbs and wondered — if he had the time — which way he should spring to get beyond the line of fire.

★ ★ ★

The first shot when it came was every bit as startling to Jim as his previous

116

shocks. It came from the fringe of the trees behind him, just at the time when he was gripping his Winchester and thinking of making a bound away from the fire in the direction which Charlie had taken.

The echoes were dinning in his ears by the time he realised that it was not aimed at him or the fire, but at the scrub patch on the other side. Instead of getting his feet under him and bounding away from his blanket, he rolled to one side, making a move of between six and eight feet.

More shots followed, and this time he had a brief glimpse of red flame from Charlie's rifle muzzle. Jim crawled then with his heart thumping and a great feeling of renewed hope in spite of the invidiousness of his position.

'Make for a fallen log, Jim, an' then turn this way. After the log, keep a-comin' fast!'

There was no mistaking Charlie's voice, charged with excitement. It had the effect of precipitating the return fire. For the first time, those who had planned the ambush opened up. Two rifles slammed bullets into the trees all around the spot where the hostile shots had come from.

Jim made three yards, thumping his right knee cap on a small unyielding rock. He was breathing hard when the third rifle, in the hands of a man not so easily diverted, started to pump shells at his line of retreat. The first bullet kicked up dust in his face; left him tasting sandy soil. He blundered on, suddenly flexed his stomach muscles too late, knowing that another shell had passed under him.

Two more whining shells were a little high, and then he had contacted the fallen tree with his forehead. He paused, half-stunned and gasping for breath. After rubbing his forehead and feeling the bark of the fallen bole, he realised what had happened. He turned resolutely towards the sharp moonlit silhouette of the trees and kept going in that direction.

Somehow he achieved a useful rhythm of movement which did not disturb the grass and fern around him. With a sudden crash the gun duel started again. This time he was left out of the reckoning. Charlie fired steadily, emptying a whole magazine over a narrow area. As he paused, the other marksmen probed his position.

There were no voices, only the bark of the discharged weapons, the whine of the projectiles on the move and the slight sounds they made when they encountered some obstruction. Jim increased his speed, but the trees seemed infinitely far away.

He called sharply, between bouts of firing: 'Charlie, are you there?'

After a brief pause, the answer came from right ahead of him.

'Keep comin' jest as you are, Jim. I can keep track of you. If I stop shootin', them jaspers down there might try to pin us down in the trees!'

Jim wanted to break off and to take a hand. He felt better disposed towards

Charlie than he had ever been since they met. Charlie *needed* some support. Jim debated with himself whether he should hole up for a bit and aim a few shells himself.

Two things prevented him from doing so. One was a distinct notion that not all the weapons which had been firing from the scrub were still in action. The other was that Charlie had asked for him to keep moving and in these circumstances he ought to have things the way he wanted them.

Jim crawled on. Charlie suddenly materialised from behind a tree and gripped him by the arm. Not bothering about whether they were in cover or not, they indulged in a firm handclasp. Charlie still had the initiative. He led the way towards the two restless horses, and Jim saw that he was as prepared as possible for instant departure.

'You've been clearin' things away while I slept, you ornery critter,' Jim complained. 'All I need for a full kit is that great blanket of mine an' the saddle. We ain't goin' back for the saddle, are we?'

Charlie chuckled and shook his head. 'You'll have to get used to ridin' without a saddle tonight, Jim. It won't be very comfortable, but it'll be better than ridin' with a butt full of bullet holes!'

Jim flinched as he brushed against the hot barrel of Charlie's gun. Three widely spaced rifle shots, fired high into the trees, prevented further comment. Jim accepted a boost on to the grey's blanketed back and prepared to depart. Charlie heaved himself up on the pinto's back and made a rude noise in the direction of the camp and beyond.

'I'll lead the way, if you're sure you can keep up ridin' Injun style,' Charlie remarked lightly.

Jim gave him his head, and concentrated on avoiding low tree branches while the timber was still about them. Their attackers must have known that they were pulling out, but the attack seemed to have faded altogether.

Charlie began to whistle quietly as the dark ground up ahead accepted them into its shadow. He was still in high spirits after the way in which he had repulsed the night attackers. For the first time since the night went wild, Jim began to think clearly, to try and get things into perspective. At first, when Charlie withdrew, he — Jim — had anticipated the worst. He thought that Charlie was two-timing him at the first opportunity. But how wrong he had been! Charlie had treated the situation in the way he thought best, and all had happened as he must have hoped.

While Jim was weighing up the action, Charlie called back: 'Sorry I didn't warn you earlier, but I thought if I tossed a pebble at you and you suddenly started wriggling when they had the guns lined up on you, you'd be blasted for certain! I had to take a chance!'

'You did it for the best, Charlie. No need to discuss it now! Press on!'

Charlie had done his work well. Whoever had planned the attack had been thoroughly thwarted. What Charlie did not know was that he had probably been firing upon his own relations, men he had ridden with for a long time. In so doing, he might have put the other Garnetts against him for all time.

Jim had a strong feeling that Charlie had become a sort of puppet of fate. He was getting a series of raw deals, and this time he was building up serious trouble for himself without having any sort of an inkling about it.

Where would it all end?

★　★　★

Behind them, Matt Garnett's action discipline delayed a movement towards the fire for almost ten minutes. He and his brothers needed the fire as a base for strapping up Drag's grooved left hip. A stray bullet had caught him in the scrub at a time when Charlie was merely seeking to keep them from advancing.

They, too, had deep cause for concern. At the outset, when Charlie moved away from the camp, they felt sure that it was their cousin they were dealing with, and that he was still acting in their best interests.

Now, however, since the ambush had been thwarted, they were angry and they did not know quite what to think. Drag, who had perhaps the best night vision, swore that the man who had scuttled away was not his cousin. Lee remained non-committal and Matt kept his thoughts to himself. He was still convinced that they were dealing with Charlie, but he had no means of knowing why he seemed to be acting in favour of Bayles.

9

The whole of the lower half of Jim Bayles' body ached unceasingly after several hours of night travel and nearly another day on horseback without the aid of a saddle. He was fast losing his enjoyment in horse riding when Charlie detected the distant sound of running water at a lower level, some little distance ahead of them, late the following afternoon.

Ever since the night encounter they had been heading south. Somewhere in that wilderness of Texas, west of the Pecos and north of the Rio Grande and Mexico, lay an explanation of what had happened two years previous. If there was any explanation at all.

Jim's zest for the truth had been blunted in the time he had ridden the grey without a saddle. Charlie had on two occasions offered to change mounts with him, but the young journalist had stoically remained on the stallion's back, taking the punishment which its heaving flanks gave out until he felt that he had taken all he could.

'Runnin' water,' Jim murmured. 'I don't suppose we'll be lucky enough to find a discarded saddle, in firstclass order, lyin' on the bank of that water, whatever it is. Me, I've jest about run out of steam for this ride around and that's the truth!'

Charlie chuckled. He felt mischievous enough to reveal his own high spirits so as to make Jim feel even worse, but a glance into his companion's grim face made him desist.

The pretty girl sitting the big roan amid the trees on the leafy-timbered slope above the wide creek seemed to Jim like a mirage. Charlie did not know what a mirage was because he had never heard of one, but he, too, thought that she was unreal at first.

She was tall and shapely with long golden hair which hung down to her shoulders from under the grey big-brimmed hat which looked like a copy of a Confederate trooper's campaign hat. Her blue eyes were wide apart and smiling, or so it seemed to the tired wanderers, seeing her for the first time.

When she really smiled, her full lips parted and showed good white teeth. Her tunic had a double row of buttons over her full breast. It was grey in colour and again suggested sympathy with the old Confederacy cause. Her long legs were sheathed in grey tight pants and ended in shiny half-boots without the benefit of spurs.

The roan shifted sideways. Fifteen feet away, the newcomers halted, rendered suddenly aware of their dishevelled clothes and the dust and perspiration which they had acquired.

'Good day to you, gents. I'm Mary Lafitte. Welcome to Sundown Creek. I live here with my father, who is retired now, and two of his old friends.'

Jim touched his hat, and Charlie was glad for him to take the initiative here.

'Good day to you — er — Miss Lafitte. This is my friend and riding pardner, Charlie Crease. My name is Jim Bayles. I believe I've met a person of your name before. Was your father ever in the army?'

The girl chuckled. She pushed back her bell of hair towards the nape of her neck. 'He surely was in the army. Almost everyone who knows him knows that. Captain Philip Lafitte, he'll say, if he likes you, and then he'll do all in his power to have you stay with us as long as possible.'

Charlie whistled and at once blushed. Jim gave out with a noisy relaxing laugh. 'Captain Phil Lafitte, of course. He was in the army an' then he set up in southern Texas as an enquiry agent of some sort.'

'Until he had a bad accident fallin' from a horse,' Mary went on, more soberly. 'An' now he's takin' things easy in Sundown Creek. Let's go see if he's back at the shack.'

The shack in question was a large

wooden cabin with extensions in the shape of extra rooms on three of its sides. The owner was not at home, and this afforded the newcomers some relief. Mary saw their embarrassment and pointed the way to a small inlet where the menfolk often bathed. It was recommended as a place where they could clean up and soak the aches out of their bones.

★　★　★

After the initial shock, the waters of the creek which were never still had a soothing effect upon the new arrivals. Five yards apart, they stood looking down through the intense greenness, watching the way the current tugged at the wilting streamers of moss.

'You said you knew the owner of this little estate, Jim. What is he like? Will he be of assistance to you?'

Jim shrugged. 'He's a rather tough-soundin' ex-military man, gettin' on in years, an' bitterly disappointed about the way the war finished. He was a good officer in his time. Everybody would agree to that. Jest how good an investigator he turned out to be in private practice I don't know.

'I don't think he'll be of much help to me as far as information is concerned, but it sure is a good thing to have a friendly callin' place in these parts, especially after what's been happenin' to us lately.'

The bathing was terminated when the partners noticed two elderly men standing amid the nearest trees and quietly contemplating them. These two threw them towels and came to meet them as soon as they had clothed themselves.

Jim judged them both to be around the fifty mark. Clear of the trees they looked younger. The man who intimated that he was Sergeant Tom Fay was short, rotund, bespectacled and bald. He covered his baldness with a smart narrow-brimmed hat made entirely out of snakeskin. His shirt was of the collarless type and his trousers looked like old army issue.

Corporal Saul March was lean and tall with a nose and jaw which would have done justice to Mr Punch. He was dressed similarly to his friend, except that his hat was made out of straw.

'The Captain said for you to come up to the house and take a drink before dinner, gents,' Fay explained, when the introductions were over.

The bathers eagerly accepted, hoping to make a good impression on the old man who ruled the local area. March and Fay took away their hard-worked horses and studied them critically for strains. Mary Lafitte met them at the nearest door of the house, smiling and smoothing down the front of her becoming blue dress.

'Welcome to our home, gentlemen. My father is waiting for you.'

Jim murmured thanks and followed her into the biggest room in the building. They found it tastefully furnished with pleasant coloured curtains and easy chairs and a long settee finished in a floral design. Captain Philip Lafitte occupied one end of the settee. His neatly trousered legs ended in black leather shoes resting on a small wooden footstool.

He was square-jawed; heavily jowled. His thick-set figure, ponderous in the waist and abdomen, made him seem older than his sixty years. His grey hair was parted high. Sideburns pointed at the ends gave him a slightly Prussian appearance which he knew about and nurtured.

He nodded to his guests, and the smile he conjured up did a lot to take the apparent frostiness out of his cold grey eyes.

'Come right in and sit yourselves down, gentlemen. You're welcome to what we have here in Sundown Creek. My daughter you've already met, an' she tells me your names are Bayles and Crease. I'm happy to know you.'

Jim hurried over to the old man so that he would not have to get up. It was clear, before they had been in the room very long, that Captain Lafitte had pains in his hips, probably resulting from his riding accident.

Jim sat in the middle of the settee, and Mary went out to fetch a tray of drinks. She came back with sherry and port and did not settle down until all three men had a glass each and were comfortably settled.

By that time, Lafitte had intimated that he often read Jim's articles and he had recollected the other time when their paths had crossed. Charlie was no sort of a house conversationalist. He was content to sit back while the old man talked about how they had first come to the creek and decided to build a house and settle there. All the felling of the trees and most of the rough building work had been done by his two old retainers Fay and March. As he talked he warmed to the two soldiers who had stayed with him after his army time was over.

Appropriately enough, they came

into the house while he was talking and he was able to formally introduce them.

'Will you stay in here with us tonight an' take wine, men?' Lafitte invited.

Charlie felt himself hoping that they would stay and that he would have a chance to talk to them, but again Sergeant Fay spoke up for the two of them.

'Thanking you, sir, but if you have no objection, the corporal an' me would prefer to take our meal on our own as usual. We're set in our ways, you see, an' we neither of us have a taste for wine.'

Jim rose to his feet as the two old hands smiled, bowed and left the room. He had the feeling that all these characters in the house were a little unreal, that they and their manners belonged to another age and another place.

Mary, however, restored his belief in them when she sat beside him at table, taking the food from a Mexican woman cook, and spreading it around the plates with a good deal of feminine dexterity.

The third course consisted of fruit, and it was while they were eating it that a rather basic question was asked.

Mary blushed as she spoke. 'I hope you gents don't think I'm sort of forward in askin' but we don't get many visitors in these parts. I was wonderin' what it was that brought you our way.'

Lafitte chuckled. 'Her mother was always like that. Curious about the menfolk. It's a trait women have, but endearin', don't you think?'

Jim nodded and Charlie smiled.

Jim said: 'All the time we're travellin' I'm on the lookout for interestin' newspaper material, Miss Mary, but I do have a special reason for bein' in these parts. Since my brother disappeared two years ago, things have never been the same for me. If only I knew what had happened to him I'd feel better.'

Jim would have gone on, but Mary, clearly, did not know the details of Hector, or his disappearance. The old man, on the other hand, made a big effort to remember and presently his grey eyes were flashing with interest. Jim produced the photograph of Hector to help him remember.

'Of course, of course, the Garnett business two years back,' Lafitte enthused. 'That was shortly before I retired from business and came here to settle. No one ever did find what happened to him, or to the money that the outlaws had hidden away in these parts.

'You may be interested to know that I tried to follow up the trail of your brother during our first few months here, but I'm sorry to say that nothing came of it. Mary, bring me that album I made the notes in.'

The chairs were pushed back and certain notes and newspaper cuttings which the captain had collected were perused over coffee and cigars. So keen was the old man on his memories and records that it was not until Charlie, Jim and he were seated on a bench against one of the outer walls, talking and smoking, that Lafitte could finally be coaxed into giving his version of the mystery.

He was slow to begin. 'I like to come out here in the evenings when the weather's good. Under the sky and the trees my memory seems to work better, too. Now, about that brother of yours. Hector, wasn't he? I think it's true he came as near as anyone to wiping out the Garnetts after that dastardly strike when they snatched the Western Settlers Association funds from the Maverick branch.

'Where he is now is a matter for conjecture. However, I suppose you'd like me to give my conclusions. Maybe you won't thank me for it, so I won't keep you in suspense. I believe he's either dead or out of this country. Out of the United States, I mean.

'I've actually been to a small isolated dwelling where Hector Bayles and another rider were supposed to be headed for. Reluctantly, I have to tell you I found no signs there.'

137

Lafitte paused for a moment and glanced up at Jim's face. 'I can see you're dismayed, but that you still have hope left. If you so desire I can direct you to the spot I've jest been talking about. Not that I'd want to go myself. Not in my present state of health.

'You'll recollect that the border with Mexico is less than two full days' ride south of here. There are settlements, of course, this side of the Rio Grande, but Casagrande is the only one I know well. It has a mixed community of white Americans and Mexicans, as you might expect.

'The dwelling that Bayles and another posse rider were supposed to be headed for is in a valley some four or five miles south-east of the town. It even had a name some years ago. The man who built it called it Waterend, because the creek which provided the water suddenly dried up for a section and made it necessary for him to do a horseback journey to quench his thirst.'

Lafitte slowed down and became

more thoughtful.

'If the search of the place doesn't amount to anything, I hope you won't feel too let down. Come back here an' stay with us for a few days, if you feel like droppin' the search. We're isolated and we need visitors. My daughter, in particular.'

Jim smiled and nodded. He examined the tip of his cigar and glanced sideways at Charlie. 'I shan't be too disappointed. I think my hopes of findin' Heck were blighted long before I came here, sir, but I do have to go on lookin' for a while longer. Maybe I'll soon have the searchin' out of my system. Then I can think of settlin' somewhere permanently.'

Shortly afterwards, Mary came out with a walking stick for her father and the four of them went for a short slow stroll around the near end of the valley. Jim and Mary strolled ahead, and while they were talking lightly of this and that, Jim felt an urge to write of other, more pleasant things, than his usual provocative articles.

He went to the room he was to share with Charlie knowing that if he stayed in Sundown Creek he would not experience loneliness.

10

'There it is, then,' Matt remarked, as he sat with his right leg draped round his saddlehorn. 'Casagrande. Quite a tidy little place. Maybe five hundred inhabitants. Mostly white Americans, but quite a few score Mexicans. Give me the spyglass, Lee.'

Matt coaxed his palomino a few feet sideways so as to reach for the spyglass from his brother. Lee, forking a claybank, patiently pulled out the glass to its full length before surrendering it. The three of them were sitting their horses on a fern-strewn rocky outcrop, looking down upon the small near-border town of Casagrande from the west.

Lee slowly dismounted. Drag, whose grooved left hip troubled him when he was riding, contented himself by shifting his newly acquired buckskin

141

into the scant shade and massaged his painful area. Lee rolled a smoke.

'Oughtn't we to go to that other spot, out in the country, first?' Drag queried. 'Waterend, I mean?'

'Why?' Matt replied bluntly.

Drag seethed. 'Because you said Bayles an' his pardner would be goin' there an' I can't wait to salivate the jasper who dug this groove in my hip. Is that sufficient of an excuse?'

Drag sounded so incensed that Matt lowered the glass from his eye and gave him a long glance of appraisal. Lee was also impressed, and he waited to see if Drag's outburst was spent.

'Would you still want revenge if you found Charlie was ridin' with that fellow, an' that Charlie was the one to shoot you?' Matt probed.

Drag slid to the ground and winced. 'Aw, you're only tryin' to make me angry! Revenge is revenge whoever it is! Why should I hold back from shootin' the fellow if I found it was cousin Charlie? Of course I'd shoot him! He deserves it, behavin' the way he has since that business at the ghost town!'

Matt became silent, his interest being solely focused on what was going on in the distant township. The time was mid-morning and the sun was strong. What he was seeing brightened him up considerably.

'Last night, before we turned in, we all agreed that we would make some sort of a strike against Casagrande,' Lee pointed out. 'Some sort of action for profit to get our hands in again. After all, we've not done ourselves any favours at all, other than to steal three horses. So why do you start belly-achin' now, brother?'

Drag gave himself a drink from his canteen. He wiped his mouth roughly on the sleeve of his shirt and then turned to see if Lee expected an answer.

'Don't take any notice of me. Maybe I'm runnin' a touch of fever on account of this burn on my hip. All right, so we hit Casagrande. How's it goin' to be done, an' what part do *I* have to play?'

'That's better,' Matt muttered, as he slipped to the ground and surrendered the glass to Lee. 'You'd better both take a good look at what is goin' on over there, an' then I'll tell you about my plan.'

Casagrande was an interesting town for its size. It had its quota of false fronts and crude shacks, but some of its main buildings erected around the Spanish-style square and adjacent church were made of neatly trimmed stone. Their green and red roof tiles gave them a bright appearance even through a spy-glass.

The steady movement of people through the streets, the square and the alleyways had only served to confirm to Matt that the town was holding a celebration of some sort. In the meadows above the town, the mixed population was indulging in games of skill and chance. The main square, however, was still the focal point, and on this occasion it was lined around the perimeter with stalls of various kinds, mostly manned by Mexican stall-holders.

While Lee and Drag were wrangling over the use of the spyglass, Matt's agile mind was busy. Any sort of a strike against a bank or other prominent building without first being acquainted with a town was asking for trouble. Here, with everyone spending freely on a day of fiesta, a lot of the town's money would be going to the stall-holders. *That* was the place to strike, but when? What time of day?

★　★　★

Towards two o'clock in the afternoon, the trio were riding down a slope which led directly into the lower half of the town. Matt was going over his last instructions.

'You, Drag, cut off as soon as we get among the streets. Visit one of those shops in the white American section to the north and come away with as much useful ammunition as you can without causing any sort of commotion.

'Of course, if you were able to create any sort of a diversion as you came away that would be all right. But don't forget our main business is with those fat greasers in charge of the stalls. It's *their* money we'll be bringin' away with us if all goes well.

'We won't strike until we've been in town for a half-hour. When we come out we'll take the southern route an' turn off to the east along the first quiet track on that side. Is that understood, Drag?'

Drag chuckled, having recovered his good spirits. Three minutes later, they parted.

★　★　★

Matt had chosen his time well. Most of the inhabitants had been far more active than usual during the forenoon and, consequently, many more of them than usual were availing themselves of a siesta in the early part of the afternoon. Provided nothing happened to give the alarm, the trio could do a great deal of damage and be clean away before the town became busy again.

Drag went into action at once. He prepared a pile of ammunition boxes and several other useful items in the centre of the counter in the biggest store which was open. As soon as the merchant started to count up the amount of the purchases, however, the outlaw realised that he was in trouble.

Not enough cash. He put on an elaborate act, claiming that he had left most of his money in the saddle pocket of his mount. Grinning broadly, he made his excuses. 'Sorry, mister. If you'd be kind enough to leave these purchases right where they are I'll go get the money an' be back in ten minutes. How will that do you?'

The shop-keeper, who would have liked an afternoon sleep like most of his rivals, yawned, but he managed to put a smile on his face and assured Drag that all would be well when he came back with the cash.

Fifty yards down the street, the outlaw saw a fat, well-dressed man taking his nap on a sidewalk bench. By the smell of him, the sleeper had partaken of a liquid lunch. His brown suit was an expensive one, and the wallet which swelled his back pocket was quite a sight for a man who had once been adept at picking pockets. Here was the answer to Drag's problem. He moved up without disturbing the sleeper, awaited his chance and then grabbed for the pocket.

His movements were deft enough, but they coincided with a restless movement on the part of the victim, who promptly rolled off the bench and woke himself up just as Drag was stepping clear with his wallet. The drunk sat up and pointed at him. Drag merely touched his hat and made for the nearest door beyond.

Unfortunately, the drunk was as touchy about his back pocket and his wallet as some men were about their guns and holsters. He emitted a sharp cry as Drag went through the door, and two or three fairly wide-awake characters took up the cry and ran after him.

It was dark in the long, rambling building. As soon as Drag had finished blinking, his eyes started to function. By the light of a distant lamp he could see that he was at the back of the seating area of the town's theatre. Instead of plunging forward down the building in the direction of the stage, he went away to his right, along the back line of seats, until he was handy for the second door.

As his pursuers rushed in, calling angrily and winning support from someone hidden behind the curtain onstage, Drag slipped out again, removed his hat and made his way back in the direction from which he had started. The robbed man was on his knees, but he turned and gave Drag a sharp glance as he came up with him.

'Which way did he go, old timer?'

The victim blinked and failed to recognise him. He pointed in the direction of the theatre, and Drag at once set off in that direction. Although he lacked an analytical brain, he had plenty of nerve. Moreover, he was remembering what brother Matt had said to him about creating a diversion. He thought he had the inkling of a useful idea along those lines.

The victim stayed in the open as though he did not trust the empty theatre. Drag went in again and walked this time down the side aisle towards the hanging lamp. As he reached up for it, those who had raced in earlier began to come through the safety curtain, wondering whether their quarry had slipped out of doors again.

'Try the dressin' rooms,' Drag bellowed. 'He has to be up that end somewhere! No one's come out of this end at all!'

The other pursuers took his advice. He promptly lowered the lamp and pulled the warm glass chimney out of position. It was the work of a moment to splash lamp oil on the curtains and then he was moving along a line of chairs. He poured the rest of the oil along the floor, splashing some of the chairs as well.

As soon as the reservoir was empty he applied the lighted wick to the spilled oil and backed away hurriedly. There was just time to apply a match to the curtains and then he had to be on his way. This time, on the sidewalk, several men had collected and they looked considerably more on the alert than those who had gone inside.

'Help, you men,' Drag called to them, 'some pickpocket has set fire to the theatre! Get the fire brigade! Tell the authorities!'

He pushed through them and made his way back to the shop where his merchandise awaited him, hurriedly shifting dollar bills from the wallet to his pocket. At last he reached the shop. He mopped his brow as he stepped inside, and handed the empty wallet to the shop-keeper.

'There's a fire down the street,' he explained, 'an' some poor fellow dashin' along there to take a look at it seemed to have dropped his wallet. I'll leave it with you, if you like.'

The merchant thanked him for his honesty and hurriedly passed over the goods to him because he was extremely keen to close his shop and go off down the street to take a look at the current excitement. Drag then slowed down, drank a couple of beers in quick succession, and returned to his mount which by then was pawing the ground and looking ill at ease on account of the nearby building with the glow of flames inside it.

Avoiding the spirited team of horses which pulled the town's water pump, Drag mounted up, turned into the next street and slowly made his way towards the square and the lower part of town. His wound was still a bit on the tacky side, but the recent action had made him forget it.

★ ★ ★

Matt started to make his strike a few minutes earlier than he had planned. On one side of the square were three merchants who appeared to be much more prosperous than the others. This trio had sold quite a fair proportion of their goods in the morning.

Others, not sleeping so well, had a broody look about them, as though they needed to do a lot better when the sun had gone down before they achieved a good day's trading.

The two plotters stood for a while in the scant shade of a dry-boled palm tree which grew at an angle from the vertical. It was more or less in the middle of the square and afforded anyone under it a useful view of all sides.

'Those three over there,' Matt was whispering. 'The fat man with the leather goods and the stalls either side of him.'

'The owners are all seated behind their stalls,' Lee pointed out unnecessarily.

'We walk along in front of the stalls an' see if there is any reaction. With those steeple hats on, you can never tell whether they're asleep or awake. Don't make it look too obvious. We make the strike in any case from the other side of the stalls.'

'From the *back*?' Lee queried.

Matt wanted a quiet operation. If anything went wrong when they were holding up the owners in front their presence would be too obvious. No one stirred as they made a closer tour of inspection. Five minutes dragged along as they moved behind the stalls and picked out the ones intended for special attention.

Matt's leather merchant had a fat head on a fat neck over a very corpulent body. His decorated steeple hat still seemed outsized for him, and the outlaw leader was unnerved because he couldn't be sure about his man. As soon as he stepped from behind the rear canvas, however, he knew what to do. He lifted the big hat and hit the man hard at the back of his skull with the butt of his revolver.

The hardest part of the operation was in preventing the limp bulk from slipping off the broad bench to the ground. Breathing hard, Matt stretched him out and put the hat over his face. The money was in a large canvas bag.

Lee's first victim came awake as he entered from the rear and laughingly redirected him around the front of the stall. Partially unnerved and on edge, Lee came back at him from the same place and drove a knife through his rib cage, penetrating his heart from the rear. The victim flopped forward in a sitting position over the counter and Lee left him there.

He collected the takings and moved along the line to the third victim. This man was really sleeping well, so Lee left him, but while he was emptying the contents of the cashbox into a bag he had acquired earlier, a sudden uproar from the north end of town roused him and made him sit up.

Men were shouting: 'Fire, fire!'

Lee also listened and had not his second victim been startled by the look on his face and possibly his red moustache, the alarm must have been given. The outlaw lunged and stabbed him as the man lurched to his feet. He had a stricken look in his dark luminous eyes which troubled Lee a little before his dead weight pulled against the blade and allowed it to be withdrawn.

On all sides now, men were beginning to arouse themselves and talk about the smoke billowing above the north of the town. Matt and Lee collected a few steeple hats and fine ponchos before they returned to their horses and slowly started to make their way out of town.

'I hope that smoke isn't Drag's idea of a diversion,' Lee murmured, when his breathing had eased.

Matt did not bother to reply, but the flinty look in his watchful eyes suggested that he would not be at all surprised if such were the case.

11

The outlaw trio boldly rode clear of the Casagrande area in steeple hats and ponchos. Although they were visible from a distance, no one took any notice because it was thought that the villains were white Americans in the cow-punchers' traditional trail garb.

Matt carried out his plan, and his party was well down a minor track towards the south-east before the sun started to dip. So flushed were they with success that they did not spend a great deal of time in looking around for an ideal camping site. A small pond served them and they relied to some extent upon the supplies of fresh water which they carried with them.

Drag roused with the sun and had his healing wound dressed by the time his brothers' coffee thirst started to inter-fere with their sleep. Although he had told them all about his off-the-cuff exploits in upper Casagrande, Matt and Lee wanted to think that he had exaggerated. They could not deny that he had started the fire, because he had the faint smell of oil upon him and the way he told his story could scarcely have been invented.

Drag moved around whistling to himself and building up the fire to a worthwhile glow for breakfast purposes. They had no reason to hurry, but the consumption of the bacon rashers was done in a standing position. Their spirits were high, and Matt did not want to do anything to dampen them. He did, however, feel that there was no earthly good in visiting Waterend for the second time. Except for revenge.

He said as much, but agreed to seek out the location when the other two insisted. To their surprise, they were mounted up for less than an hour when their leader called a halt and asked for the spyglass. Lee handed it over and at once started standing up in the saddle.

Matt was the only one who had visited the isolated location known as Waterend, and his brothers were consumed with curiosity.

'Any signs of life?' Drag asked bluntly.

Matt did not answer and Lee reckoned he could not see well enough with the naked eye. Ahead of them, the ground dropped away smoothly and without any sharp descents. The side of one hill came in first on their right, which was to the south. On the opposite side, the north, a longer more gentle slope appeared to overlap the first one at valley floor level because of a natural undulation.

A double line of dwarf pines halved the middle distance, and beyond the trees and as far again an old splitlog cabin nestled in a sparse tree copse with foliage hiding its sloping roof. Originally, it had been rather a long building, but since the original builder had had it someone had added another room down one long side so that now, seen from above, it resembled in plan a letter 'T'.

Matt breathed out rather heavily and handed over the spyglass. Drag got it first this time and Lee was the one who had to wait.

'Do you have an answer to your own question yet?' the latter asked, twisting his ginger moustache.

'No, I don't see any signs of anyone there, but I have me a feelin' about it. Here, you take a look. Maybe you'll pick out something I've missed.'

Drag surrendered the glass and dismounted. He tugged a few handfuls of lush bunch grass and fed them to his buckskin. While he was doing so he eyed Matt speculatively. 'Are you sure that's the cabin you searched previously?'

Matt gave him an arch look. 'Sure enough that's the spot. The one I visited, I mean. Our adopted brother, Sam, was supposed to bury the whole of the loot single-handed in a cellar under an extra room or stable. As you'll have seen, that dwellin' place has an extra room of some sort, but there's no cellar underneath it. No cellar at all. *I* know. I've searched, an' I'm not the one to overlook a cache of loot.'

Lee lowered the spyglass but stayed in the saddle a while longer.

He remarked: 'It is a great pity we never made contact with Sam after we scattered. Still, he was always very much in favour of the family. He never forgot our old man took him in when he had nowhere to go. I don't think he'd keep it for himself.'

'Nor would he give it to anyone else!' Matt added sharply.

'How can you be sure that there's no cellar anywhere there?' Drag put in brusquely.

'As you'll see when you get there, you impatient jasper, that room has a beaten-earth floor! Maybe the sight of it will convince you!' Matt spat tobacco juice out of the side of his mouth. He was quietly mouthing imprecations when he hit the ground and walked about impatiently. After a while, he resumed: 'As you were sayin', Lee, it's a pity we never had Sam back with us, but I don't have any reason to doubt that he met with a perfectly unavoidable accident.

'The way I heard it from a stranger, his horse tripped and pitched him down a crevice. This hombre went to a deal of trouble to bring his body up to the surface again an' bury him. I reckon I know he was speakin' the truth.'

'So you think that's the spot,' Drag murmured, 'an' almost certainly there's nothin' there for the finding.'

'That's about the size of things, boys,' Matt replied calmly. 'I didn't want you to get worked up about loot when I agreed to come this way jest once more.'

'Maybe we ought to put that old loot out of our heads for ever,' Drag muttered morosely.

'Would it make any difference to us if there was somebody in residence?' Lee wondered.

Matt hurried over to him. 'You ain't foolin', are you, boy?'

'Nope, I'm not foolin', brother. Use my saddle. Take a look for yourself!'

Matt did just that. A mere half-minute in the saddle with the glass to his eye was sufficient to put a rather forbidding smile upon his lips. All he could see was smoke coming from the chimney, but that was enough.

Now, for the first time on this speculative journey, he thought a visit to Waterend was worth while. 'Mount, boys, we're goin' closer. When we get through that timber along there, we'll rein in an' take another look. After all, if we have the two riders up in front that we're keen to meet, we don't want to warn them in advance, do we?'

★ ★ ★

Neither Jim nor Charlie had slept well in the abandoned cabin known as Waterend. They had used the original part of the building for their dining and

163

sleeping room and the extra room was not used by them at all.

After a restless night they both slept longer than was usual, and a feeling of futility made them reluctant to get up from their temporary bunks. Charlie had been more silent than of late before they turned in. On arrival at the lonely shack he had expected some sort of a development in their relationship and their search, but clearly Jim was very disappointed.

The sheer lack of clues to anything that might have happened in the past had disheartened him. Jim felt sure that he had found the proper location, as outlined by Captain Lafitte, and he could see now why the old man had been rather disappointed in his own private investigations into the disappearance of Heck Bayles.

Charlie made an effort. He sprang up off his bunk and threw a few chunks of logs into the stove which was centrally placed. With his thumbs in his gun belt, he kicked a little life into the heap of ashes which had sunk down to the bottom during the night. A few sparks greeted his efforts, and although the morning was a warm one the pair of them felt an inner sense of warmth out of all proportion to the temperature.

Charlie examined his chin in a mirror nailed to one wall. At the same time he regarded his travelling companion. Jim looked troubled.

'You want I should get you a cigar, amigo?' Charlie offered.

'I have one in my pocket, thanks. I don't suppose it's any news to you that I'm bitterly disappointed in the spot, Charlie. I came along with great hopes even though old Lafitte warned me not to get too keyed up. You know what we did before we turned in. Do you think there is any further need for searchin' or should we move on fairly soon?'

Charlie shrugged at the mirror. He thought that in doing so he cut a rather comic figure, but this was not the time for fooling about. He thought seriously about what Jim had said and tried to give advice.

'Jim, that sort of decision ought to be yours. Me, I'm disappointed because you are. So what can I say?' He pointed with his thumb towards the extra room. 'We didn't give that place much of a goin' over, did we?'

Jim sniffed, and pushed an elbow under him. 'I don't think there's anything to be learned by the out-of-doors. I mean there's nothin' and no one buried among the trees. At least, I'd gamble there isn't. And this main section of the buildin' an' the loft look pretty straightforward to me. As you say, we didn't give that other bit much of a search, though. As far as I was concerned, it seemed to repel me. I had a feelin' I can't describe.'

He paused, grimaced and drew thoughtfully on his cigar.

'Hell an' tarnation,' Charlie blurted out, 'so you had that feelin' too, did you? I wonder what caused it? Originally, somebody built on that extra room for a bedroom or a livin' room, but in recent years it looks as if it might have been used for a stable! That's something of a change, ain't it?'

Jim nodded. 'You're goin' by that end wall. Somebody did away with the original door an' put in a bigger one. I noticed that, too.'

'There is jest one other thing which puzzled me about that extension,' Charlie murmured, with his hands planted on his hips.

Jim blew hot ash off his shirt and waited for Charlie's pronouncement. He had no great hopes of a special revelation, but he was in for a surprise.

'It used to have a wooden floor. Not that that has to be at all significant. But at the first glance that beatenearth surface looks as if it might have been there as long as the building.'

Jim's brow furrowed. Charlie, watching him covertly, knew that he had given him something to think about.

'Somewhere in the back of my mind I seem to remember something about a cellar. But I might have dreamed it. I've been thinkin' about my brother's disappearance for so long that I can't tell the truth from conjecture, an' that's serious.'

Charlie moved around. He put the coffee pot on top of the stove and came to sit on the foot of Jim's bed.

'I can understand you gettin' a bit of brain fag over your surmisin', Jim. Me, I wish I could remember enough to surmise over. But that's another problem. As far as that room goes, we can get through there an' turn it over again jest as soon as you feel able.'

'Sure, sure, Charlie. I have to admire your patience on occasion. We'll wait for the coffee, then we'll take a look. I guess you must be thinkin' the same as I am. If the original floor has gone, there might have been something other than an earth floor underneath it. I know it doesn't have to be that way, but it makes a difference. Something to look into before we move on again. So how is the coffee comin' along?'

'In a few minutes,' Charlie advised.

He walked around the main room, glancing through the windows and assuring himself for the first time that morning that they had the place to themselves. He was, at the same time, trying to put himself into Jim's thoughts.

'Hadn't we better wait till after breakfast, Jim?'

Jim ducked out from the lower of the two bunks and slowly straightened up to his full height. It did not take him long to figure out what Charlie was thinking.

'I was only thinkin' of *lookin'* before breakfast, amigo. But thanks for your consideration. You're thinkin' about diggin' and findin'. I can guess what you have in mind.'

Soon, they were examining the extension and there was clear evidence for the finding that a floor had been laid at one time. Here and there amid the split logs of the walls and near to earth level there were small crevices with bits of timber still adhering to them which had been part of the floor.

The earth surface was good and flat. There was no sign of a depression in it anywhere. Five minutes of studying it was as much as either of them wanted to give before they partook of their food. The meal preparation was done between them. As they sat on opposite sides of the table, eating steadily and swilling their food down with coffee, they regarded each other steadily without embarrassment.

Jim eventually raised his brows.

Charlie said: 'If there was a cellar it would have to be several feet deep. That would mean quite a lot of diggin', if you still have that in mind.'

Jim was slow to answer. At last he sighed and pushed away his empty cup. 'I can't ask you to indulge in diggin' for hours in there, Charlie. It wouldn't be fair. Besides, a man doesn't use a first-class bodyguard that way.'

Jim grinned. Charlie took the remark the way it was intended.

'Now you're tryin' to put me off. Why, there might be a treasure worth a king's ransom down there, an' where would *I* be if you found it all yourself? Nowhere! Nowhere at all.'

Charlie dried up suddenly. They were both smiling for a while, and then their expressions changed. Again they were eyeing one another.

'I didn't really mean anything by what I said, Jim,' Charlie said quietly. 'I was only tryin' to take your thoughts off other things which might not be pleasant. You know how it is.'

'I know how it is, an' I'm grateful, Charlie. Durin' the time you've been lookin' after me I've learned some pretty good things about you. Sometimes I feel I know you really well.'

Slight embarrassment made Jim turn away. He was thinking that for an outlaw Charlie was blessed with some very desirable character traits. Charlie's close scrutiny made him blush.

12

Neither of them had ever heard of a cellar in a western shack starting anywhere but in the middle. Consequently, they started the excavation exactly in the middle of the extra room and within a half-hour, even with the outer and the inner door open, the atmosphere bore traces of their mingling perspiration.

By mutual consent they packed up for a minute or two. One took air by the outer door and the other propped himself up by the inner. On resumption, Charlie had his shirt off and he worked slower and dug harder with his implement.

Jim, whose thoughts were tormented by what they might find, was not at his best as an excavator. He had more frequent rests, and changed his stance occasionally to jab at the spade with the other foot. Charlie's more deliberate digging around the same spot made him pull out of the way.

He was straightened up and taking an unearned rest when Charlie's spade blade touched something which was not soil and not rock. Jim hurried forward to relieve him, but he was waved back.

'Brace yourself, amigo,' Charlie murmured, his breath labouring.

Anguish had already etched itself into Jim's expression. He deduced from Charlie's remark that he expected to find a body rather than a box of loot. Jim's hand shook. He dropped his spade and backed away to the nearest window, wondering if this was the end of his two years' search.

Charlie moved closer to his work. Soon, he was on his knees. To Jim he was taking all the time in the world before making any sort of pronouncement.

'Don't you have any sort of idea, Charlie?' he called out, in a voice which sounded as if his windpipe was partially impeded.

A minute later, the digger slowly straightened up with an exhibit in his hand. 'If you ask me, Jim, this is a human bone rather than that of an animal. I don't like what I'm doin', but I'll keep on for a while, for your sake, 'cause I know how you've been sufferin'. But while I'm busy why don't you take a little walk? After this, my job might be distinctly unpleasant.'

Clearly, by the look in his eyes, Charlie meant what he said. Jim studied the small bone which had been unearthed. He guessed it to be a collarbone or a part of a rib. And that was all he could stomach, thinking as he was bound to do that he might be witnessing the unearthing of his brother's remains.

Charlie scrambled to his feet and walked deliberately past him into the other room. When he returned he had his bandanna in his hand. He studied the red square, folded it in half, and before he put it across his mouth to breathe through, he turned to Jim again.

'Why don't you go an' take a look at the horses, amigo?' he pleaded.

Jim swallowed hard, hesitated and then took the hint. He went through the main part of the building and out at the other side, listening as he went for further sounds of activity from within. Soon he was out of earshot, and in order to keep himself busy until Charlie had finished with the most gruesome part of the exhumation he picked up two grooming brushes from the spot where they had dumped the saddles and went to work on the horses, brushing his own first. The grey had been a little out of sorts with itself and its rider recently. Probably it had not enjoyed the barebacked trek, or the succeeding one where Jim had perched on a borrowed saddle from the Lafittes.

He worked away with all-absorbing passion as though to drive all conjecture from his mind while Charlie was still labouring. The grey was finished and pushed aside. Charlie's low-barrelled pinto next had the treatment and this time it was not quite so thorough because Jim was wilting a little due to the unaccustomed exercise following straight after the digging.

His curiosity mounted, and soon he was retracing his steps to the building where his brother might well have died in suspicious circumstances. A brief reluctance to come to grips with the findings made him go round the outside instead of through the building. On the very threshold of the extra room he happened to look up, distantly towards the west. At once, his eyes focused upon movement in front of trees.

Three men on horses were shifting about as though restless to be on the move. Moreover, they seemed to be fooling around with headgear. Big hats, probably Mexican tall ones. There was nothing in the appearance of the strangers, particularly at that distance, to warrant any sort of panic.

Jim was surprised, though, and he ducked into the room where the digging was taking place and made known his information. 'We're under observation from the west side, near those trees! Three men mounted up an' lookin' restless, as though they might come ridin' along here any time. What do you think we ought to do?'

To Jim's surprise, he found that Charlie had been actively engaged in banging down the earth again for most of the time since he went out.

'This is an unlucky place, Jim. I say we pull out in a hurry. We've had three guns lined up on us before today an' this might be the same group trailin' us again. Let's put our things together an' go, huh? I know all there is to know about this grave. Jest one man buried here, an' he's not your brother. So let's hurry!'

Charlie snatched up his shirt, brushed the perspiration from his brow and hurried through the inner door. He grabbed his hat and a few other things, along with his weapons, and dashed out by another door which led away from the shack.

Twenty yards away, he paused and made sure that Jim was following him. Jim's expression showed that he was baffled, but he had accepted what Charlie had said about the dead man not being his brother. Almost certainly, new thoughts had started turning in Jim's head and the immediate planning would fall to Charlie.

Charlie went ahead and slammed two blankets on the backs of the waiting horses. The quadrupeds soon realised that they were due for a hasty departure. The grey's blanket was trailing again when Jim came up, but he made an effort of concentration and his mount was ready within a minute of Charlie's.

'South again, then, is it?' Charlie croaked wearily.

'I guess so,' Jim agreed, 'but jest for now we'll follow our noses towards the east. Let's see where this valley goes.'

Charlie set a cracking pace for men who had nowhere special to go except away. Over an hour had gone by when the track they were following showed up more clearly and began to converge with another one coming from the north-west.

And that was not all. Another party of riders was coming down that track towards the intersection. They would arrive within a few minutes. Jim reined in and glanced across at his partner.

'This time we wait and make contact. After all, this new bunch can't be the same as I saw back there. They're comin' from a new direction altogether. I say we wait an' we talk to them.'

Charlie shrugged. He crooked a leg round his saddlehorn and pushed back his hat. These days he could do that without fear of a pain in the temple. 'Okay, amigo. So now do you want me to talk about the grave back there?'

Jim groaned. 'All right, tell me how

179

you knew it was not my brother. Or did you jest say that to get me away from the place?'

Charlie looked annoyed, but his expression changed and he handed over a metal name tag on a thin chain. Jim took it and saw where Charlie had scraped the dirt off the side with the name banged into it.

'It looks like Wilbur Dyce. What do you make of that?'

'I don't know any Wilbur Dyce. I never knew anyone of that name. It might be the missing posse rider someone spoke of, or then again Dyce might be one of the owners of the shack. That's all my sort of brain can do with a problem like that. But you could ask someone else.'

Charlie turned his head towards the sounds of the approaching riders. A brief billowing cloud of dust came into view before them, and then the space between the two lines of fringe rock was full of horses and riders. A tall man in a cream side-rolled stetson with woollen chaps and a checked shirt threw up his arm and halted his outfit.

Sunlight glinted upon his star and several men at once pulled their rifles and seemed prepared for anything.

'I'm Deputy Mel Shires out of Casagrande! Raise your hands an' state your name an' occupation!'

Jim sensed rather than saw Charlie's sudden reaction to this peremptory order to put up his hands. He lifted his own and at once turned towards his partner.

'Whatever you do, don't lift a gun, amigo. Do as the man says. This is one of my sort of occasions!'

Reluctantly, Charlie hoisted his hands. As soon as that was done, Jim felt himself smouldering. 'If Abraham Lincoln came ridin' along this way backed by his followers, he would show more courtesy to law-abidin' strangers.'

Deputy Shires' grin had a wolfish quality to it. 'I'm not Abe Lincoln an' this is not Lincoln country. My town, Casagrande, has a problem on its hands. We're lookin' for murderers, an', so far, everybody we've asked has accounted for his movements. You owe me an explanation.'

'I haven't been to Casagrande and I owe you nothing, but I'll answer your question, nevertheless. My name is Jim Bayles. I write for the papers. My pardner is Charlie Crease. We're travellin' at the moment, turnin' up material on my brother, a federal marshal who disappeared in these parts. Maybe you could help me.'

Shires looked disappointed; as if he didn't want to help. As if he would have been more pleased to have apprehended more doubtful characters. Two stern-faced men close up behind him confirmed that Jim Bayles' photo looked like this man, and the rest of the posse started to relax.

Jim was the first to start to lower his hands. Charlie did the same straight afterwards. Shires wanted to chide them, but he thought better of it.

The posse lost formation. Some men

dismounted. Others drank from their canteens. A few just talked.

'Do you know anybody by the name of Wilbur Dyce? We were diggin' around at Waterend hopin' to find some clue to my brother's disappearance an' we turned up a body. It had this name tag on it.'

A leather-faced man named Tim Saddler moved forward. He appeared to know more about local events than Shires did. 'Wilbur Dyce was the name by which a posse man was known at the time Heck Bayles dropped from view. So that's where he was buried.'

Jim gave a few details, and for the first time Charlie joined in. This man Saddler did not antagonise him like the other man did. There was some discussion about the possibility of Heck's body being elsewhere in the same area, but neither Jim nor Charlie were shaken in their views that Waterend had no more secrets.

'Tell us about the murders,' Jim suggested, when he wanted the topic of conversation changed.

Shires tried to get back into the discussion, but Saddler effectively kept him out until the firing of the theatre and the sneak killings had been described in lurid detail. Shires apparently was tiring of the exchanges now. He called the other men to horse and was about to remonstrate with Saddler when the latter drew an unexpected response from Jim.

'The reason they slipped clear of town, apart from that diversion in the theatre, didn't become clear until later. They'd stolen Mexican hats from the stalls! When they rode away they were wearin' Mexican traditional head-dresses, don't you see?'

This mention of steeple hats at once jogged Jim's memory. 'In that case, I think I can tell you where to locate them. We pulled out of Waterend in a hurry because we thought we were goin' to be visited by three hostiles. I saw these men gettin' ready to ride down on the shack an' that was less than two hours ago.'

Shires walked his mount in closer. Jim had everyone's attention by this time. 'I have to tell you that you may be up against the Garnett gang. I ran into them myself up in Ghost Town Creek earlier this month. Since then our trails have crossed and they've done their best to eliminate me. Without success, largely due to Charlie's efforts. So, if you do run into these hombres, don't hesitate to fire. They're back in business an' they're quite deadly, as you know from the other. So long now, and good huntin'!'

The parting was much more cordial than the greeting at first encounter. Jim made it clear that he and his partner would still be searching for traces of his missing brother, and that his direction would be towards the border with Mexico.

As they moved off in the new direction, their topic of talk was the Garnetts and the events in Casagrande.

13

Matt Garnett was angry when he found the two men at the shack had been aware of their presence. He had tired a little of chasing Jim Bayles and he felt the time to catch up with the fellow was just about then.

Consequently, when they ringed the place, drew a blank and found that their potential victims were already a good mile away down the easterly track, he gave vent to his feelings in no uncertain manner.

'I'm not sure we shouldn't ride after them at speed,' he replied viciously, when Lee remarked that the shack might prove a useful hideout for a day or two.

'You're frustrated, brother,' Drag pointed out. He was exhibiting a boldness he would not have dared show before the events in Casagrande. 'Jest because this Bayles hombre is provin' elusive, you shouldn't ought to let him get you down. Ain't that good advice?'

He glanced around, seeking confirmation. Lee avoided his gaze and Matt gave him a look which would have terrified many a casual passer-by.

'All right, then, jest this one more time we let them get ahead of us. But we ain't goin' to waste our time around this place. We use it and we move on. Firstly, we need to know what it was in that extension which held two men's interest for so long, and then allowed them to clear out in a hurry. So let's move in an' find out.'

Within a minute they were indoors, steeple hats discarded and prowling for anything of value which the previous occupiers might have mislaid or overlooked. Matt still continued to drive his brothers and within a very short space of time they were all standing in the extra portion regarding that section of the floor which had been hurriedly hammered flat by Charlie.

'Somethin' was buried under there an' Bayles found it. He sure is a careful investigator,' Matt murmured. 'What we want to know is what it was.'

'The missin' loot that Sam was supposed to leave here?' Drag suggested in an excited voice.

'Or something else,' Lee put in dryly.

Matt knew what he was getting at. It occurred to the leader that the diggers might have found both possibilities. His growing frustration with the Bayles business made him bawl his brothers out and start them digging to find the truth.

Three of them digging and knowing where to start made the job somewhat simpler than the previous pair had had it. Drag's hip began to ache, and presently — when they had turned up a couple of bones — he made an excuse to leave the digging area and go over to the horses.

He had the feeling that Matt would find some excuse for not staying the night. This filled him with speculation as to where their next resting place was likely to be. Disliking the digging work, he decided to climb one of the trees of the copse to see what the distant vista might have in store for them.

His self-imposed climb did the hip wound more harm than the digging, but it saved all of them from falling into the clutches of the avenging posse riders. He came down much faster than he had gone up, and as he ran back to the building, dragging the horses by their head ropes, Matt and Lee came out looking amazed, but very much on the alert.

'A tight bunch of riders on their way here!' he panted. 'They have posse written all over them and they look as if they know exactly where they're goin'! If you ask me, the pair we disturbed contacted this pack and sent them after us! It stands to sense, seeing as how they're comin' up the same trail!'

For once, no one argued with him at all. They tightened up their saddles without delay, turned away from the ill-fated shack and started to put distance between it and themselves. Firstly, they had to backtrack a short way. Then, at the first opportunity, they pulled away to the south and kept going at speed for nearly two hours.

During that time, no mention was made of Drag's hip or any other sort of weakness which might have slowed them. None of them were in any doubt about the sort of reactions their quiet killings would provoke. In two years, southern Texas had begun to develop a taste for law and order.

Later, when their movement had slowed to a walk and the men had slaked their thirst, there was time for some discussion. Lee and Drag still wanted Bayles eliminated. Matt, a little longer in the tooth and still thinking that Bayles might be the key to the missing loot, went along with their wishes.

They continued to head south, although it was clear to them that they were fast running out of United States soil.

★　★　★

Around eight o'clock that evening, Jim and Charlie, who had made very steady progress all through the afternoon, came out upon the northern bank of the formidable Rio Grande river. They rode along a section of it which is normally known as the Little Bend and wondered about the possibility of crossing it without having to ride any distance to a ford or a ferry.

Their short ride alongside the roaring force of water brought them to a high flat table of rock which afforded quite a good view of the river and the rich foliage which grew thick and lush on the southern bank. Flying spray made a sort of rainbow below them and captivated them in spite of their saddle weariness.

Resting within the area of that formidable noise made a great deal of change for the wanderers. Charlie climbed down to the bank and tried his hand at fishing, while Jim carried the makings of a fire up on to the mesa and set about making a camp where they could not feel ringed in by the surrounding countryside.

This idea for a camp was a good one, but darkness was still some time away and a lot could happen before nightfall. Charlie's fishing proved hopeless in the fastmoving current, and they had to fall back upon jack-rabbit for their evening meal.

Although the water sounds persisted throughout the evening, their early enthusiasm for the special atmosphere of Little Bend underwent a gradual change. They began to think beyond the waterway, wondering what sort of living conditions obtained in the country beyond.

Ever since the war with Mexico, certain areas of the border region had been locations of unrest. The Mexicans tended to keep to themselves, and anyone who crossed openly between border posts was probably looked upon as a smuggler of something or other. By the time the food was consumed they were ready to smoke, and while the eddies from a cigarette and a small cigar were ascending in straight lines on either side of the fire, they talked.

'I wonder if you've ever crossed over this mighty river, Charlie?' Jim pondered, without thinking very clearly.

Charlie groaned, and Jim realised what he had done.

'I'm sorry, amigo, really I am,' Jim added hurriedly. 'We've been together for so long now that I had forgotten you'd lost your memory. Perhaps I ought to have said, 'Has my brother ever crossed this river?' Do you think he might have?'

Charlie shrugged off the old griping worry about his memory and tried to apply his brain afresh to Jim's enduring problem.

'He might have, and then he might not. I don't want to put you off by

193

givin' my views when you have dedicated yourself to such a detailed search. After all, you are about to cross the southern border of your own country, an' your business in life, that of writing for the newspapers, seems to have been pushed into the background.

'All I can say is that you may yet have to endure a whole lot of heartache over your brother, whether he turns up or he doesn't turn up. Alive, or not alive.'

Having said what he had in mind, Charlie rose slowly to his feet. Water, especially moving water, had never attracted him very much. The Rio Grande had more moving water than anything else he had ever seen. And it had to be crossed. It was good that others had seen the need for crossings before he and his partner came along. It was reassuring for a non-swimmer to know that others had found the best places to cross: the fords, and, where there were no fords, the ferries which crossed in the deep places.

Charlie yawned, and as his eyes came

open again he threw back his head and glanced away from the river. This was the first time that he remembered looking away from it since the first moment when they had come under its spell.

He sounded terribly sad and dispirited when he said: 'Oh, Jim, we're about to be interrupted all over again! What do we have to do to shake off that followin' trio?'

Jim only caught half of what he was saying, but he came to his feet and stood beside him, and within a minute he had picked out the small approaching cloud of dust and pinpointed the riders who came before it. The spyglass gave them no comfort. It merely confirmed their fears and left them with that unsettled feeling which assails most people who are faced with new and difficult problems late in the day.

Jim became bitter. 'We were goin' across the river, but now we have to do it in haste, an' we can't pick our spot. We were unwise to make our camp in such a prominent spot. No time to whine about that, though. Get the horses ready, Charlie, an' let's get down to the bank as soon as possible.

'All the time we have in hand is ten or fifteen minutes. And after that, if we haven't crossed, the sun is likely to complicate our movements. Somehow I can't quite visualise what it will be like to arrive in a foreign country after nightfall.'

'How do you think *I* feel, a non-swimmer?' Charlie protested bitterly.

Necessity made them go through the motions of breaking camp and moving down to the lower level. Jim had already weighed up the waters and the girth of the river from the top of the mesa. He knew that the crossing would be difficult, and that if they hit any special snags there would be no one to whom they could turn for help.

The point where Jim planned to cross was some two hundred yards along the bank in a downstream direction. As they rode towards it, Jim tried to give advice.

'I'll lead the way. You follow me, an' don't wait for any length of time because turbulent water like this has a way of opening up gaps between people. We need to stick with our horses an' we must get across. If the current decides otherwise we can't expect to live long when that trio hits the north bank.

'So although it looks formidable, we'll have to do it. Are you feelin' committed to the crossin'?'

Charlie was feeling more uncertain of himself than he had known since his memory left him. 'Why can't we make a run for it along the bank, till we find a ford or something, or until the darkness hides us from our enemies?'

'On this occasion, I think they'd catch us before the light went. Havin' seen us leave the mesa, they'll know we came downstream. Almost anyone would come this way instinctively, if they intended to cross. I don't really think we have an alternative, Charlie, unless we simply ride back to meet them and take a chance on blasting them before they blast us. Now, what do you say? One thing, I won't leave you.'

They were still moving towards Jim's selected spot on the river bank at some speed. It was not until they were actually on the spot that Charlie shuddered and offered his answer.

'I'll be guided by you, as always, but I don't have the know-how for makin' a good showin' in water. So I'll want plenty of advice.'

Jim nodded and grinned. He slipped to the ground and slackened his saddle girth, explaining that it would tighten up on the horse's belly due to the effects of the river water. Charlie dismounted and did the same. He appeared to be almost hypnotised by the fast-moving flow of water only a few feet away from them.

'They'll be able to shoot at us while we're still strugglin' across!'

'I know they will,' Jim shouted back again, 'but their aim will probably be spoiled by all that spray flyin' about! Now, come a bit closer! See that swirl in the water about fifty yards downstream on the other bank?'

Charlie nodded, showing no eagerness. He was thinking that it might as well be five hundred miles away, as far as he was concerned.

'That's where I'm aimin' for! We try to cut across the current, startin' from that outward juttin' portion of the bank a few yards further down. As soon as we clear that juttin' portion the struggle will be on. A lot will depend upon the horses. If one of them goes under, then we'll jest have to improvise.

'If we get swept too far down, apart from becomin' a better target, we may meet up with more unexpected rocks. Try an' keep off them if you see any I miss! Lastly, keep in the saddle, an' if that fails try an' not lose touch with the pinto. The horses won't relish the swim, but they'll probably make a better job of it than either of us.'

After checking that his equipment was as secure as he could make it, Jim patted Charlie on the shoulder and swung back into the saddle. At once he started to make encouraging noises to the big grey, on which his safety depended. Charlie mounted up as well, but he had little to say to anyone. His mouth had dried out.

Jim determinedly turned the stallion's head towards the narrowing strip of sandy soil on the river side of the spit they were standing on. Now, the tremendously powerful throb of noise was crowding every other consideration out of his mind.

He turned briefly at the last possible moment, waved encouragingly to Charlie who was crouched unhappily on the back of the pinto, and then urged the grey stallion into the water. It whinnied with terror for a few seconds and then took the plunge, going down what seemed an awful long way before its head and neck emerged and stayed up.

Charlie tried to shout to his mount and failed. His legs twitched as he communicated with his thighs and calves. The pinto, shaking its head from side to side, plunged in after the other horse. To Charlie, tensed up on its back, it seemed for a few interminable seconds that they were plunging to a watery grave.

14

The awful power of the moving body of water was a shock to Jim, a man confident in streams and creeks for as long as he could remember. To Charlie, following up behind, who had an infant's fear of water which had never been eradicated, it was like feeling the menace of the devil, the tug of hell.

Surging green water rolled over the necks of the struggling horses and forced them to greater efforts to stay afloat. The way they suffered did little to boost the confidence of their riders.

Jim fought on with a dourness born of sheer necessity. Unbelievably, his thoughts at times turned away from the immediate menace into side-channels of speculation. For instance, it occurred to him that his protracted search for his brother might very likely bring about his own premature death. What a remarkable turn of events that would be if he — Jim — died and Heck was still alive somewhere else and in the best of health!

By sheer limb power the grey stallion battled its way about a quarter of the distance across. Already, the pull of the current had sent them many yards further downstream than the point from where they had started. Jim, however, by his own performance in the saddle, did give a measure of confidence to a horse which had served him bravely in less exacting exploits.

Such was the task before him that for a while he had no chance whatever to take stock of Charlie's problems behind him. Once, when he was all set to turn around in the saddle and check on Charlie and the possible arrival of the enemy, a sudden churning in the water warned of another danger. The grey was almost literally sucked against a dark pinnacle of rock which only cleared the surface by a few inches. A terrific straining on the part of the animal, backed up by Jim, who actually stuck his left boot against the rock, had the effect of taking them clear, but only by inches.

After that, Jim was so glad to be still afloat and in touch with the stallion that he relaxed all pressure and let it have its head. Risking a sudden loss of balance such as the race around the rock created, he turned and surveyed the nearest waters upstream.

The first glance reassured him on the point that Charlie was still in with a fighting chance, but the battle his partner was making suggested that both horse and rider might fail to survive the complete crossing. Clearly, if Charlie was unhorsed, the power of the current would bring about his death before Jim could help him.

Charlie had his lower limbs locked around the barrel of the pinto and he was driving it across the current as though they were crossing a fiery cauldron. The pinto showed through the eyes that it was under severe pressure and that it could not keep up the uneven struggle much longer.

Jim yelled: 'Charlie, don't press your horse so hard, you'll kill it! Ease up a little, won't you?'

None of these words carried as far as the second rider although there was barely fifteen feet of water between them. Jim's thoughts were racing. He wanted to try and check the American bank to see if the outlaws were going up the mesa or cutting across to attack them further down the bank.

Again the river commanded attention. In a matter of seconds, the flailing forelegs of the tiring pinto had struck an underwater obstruction, the top of a rock which did not rise high enough to break the surface. The effect of the slight collision was instantaneous. Robbed of its balance, the pinto suddenly dipped down in the water and rolled over.

Charlie emitted a strangled cry which was muted and cut off by the noise of the all-embracing waters. He parted company with surprising ease, being freed from saddle and stirrups by the mightiest power he had ever experienced.

The big, undented fawn stetson, which had become so much a part of his personality since he received the head wound, parted from his head and drifted downstream like a miniature raft. Seconds went by, some of the longest seconds of Jim's life, before Charlie's head reappeared with his hair flattened but his eyes blinking.

Jim made a rapid appraisal of their position. He was several feet further across the current than Charlie and maybe ten feet downstream of him. There was little he could do of a positive nature, and yet he made his effort. Exhibiting a lot of strength and much tenacity of will, he prevailed upon the grey to stay its effort. There was a slowing of forward progress, and while the willing stallion floundered and stayed put, the pinto reappeared, shooting to the surface as though it had been ejected from some subterranean chamber by a truly dynamic force.

The pinto, relieved of its rider, bore down upon the grey, but Jim had no time to consider the animal for the moment. He was more intent upon what would happen to his non-swimming partner. He and Charlie had been together for so long now that any further search without him might seem pointless. Oddly enough, in this seething maelstrom of lethal churning water, the events which had brought them together, and Charlie's obvious beginnings in life, had no special significance.

As Jim reached out towards his struggling partner, Charlie rolled in the water. He called out in anguish, had his shout cut off as water filled his mouth, and briefly disappeared. All in a few feet he was down, over and up again.

Jim was not able to do anything to close the gap. Nor was he able to improve Charlie's chances of missing the next hazard. A rock extremity, which only showed every now and then, came steadily closer to Charlie's head. To one looking on, it seemed almost as if the rock were swimming towards the man.

Charlie turned with a great effort, as though looking for his partner. Too late, he saw the projecting rock. It was the back of his head which connected with it and momentarily slowed his progress downstream.

The grey did a kind of lurch in the water, which enabled the flagging pinto to pass right under its nose on the way across. Without its rider, it was doing better.

Jim yelled out a warning and an instruction, both of which were lost upon Charlie. His senses appeared to be reeling. All that kept him afloat as he slowly slid round the rocky projection and began to move again were his basic instincts for survival.

His hands and wrists, his straining face were all that showed as he floated, mostly submerged, towards Jim's clutching hands. The action of the water and an attack of nerves made the first two frantic grabs useless. It was at the third attempt, when Jim's confidence was rapidly going back on him, that his clutching fingers connected properly with the cloth of Charlie's shirt at the nape of his neck.

Some time later, when they were going over the hazards, they realised that a grip on the bandanna instead of the shirt might have strangled him.

Held by the neck, Charlie felt a new lease of life. He opened his eyes wide without knowing particularly what was happening to him and reached over his head to grab Jim by the leg. In that awkward position, Jim had to relinquish his handhold before he was sure whether Charlie would be able to hold on or not.

While this struggle was going on, involving two men and one horse, the other quadruped, which had seemed doomed at one time, stabbed its feet into the mud and clay of the southern bank and slowly floundered out.

A rifle fired from the top of the mesa probed its position but made no material difference to the situation. The sound of the weapon was considerably muted, and neither of the men was aware of it owing to the pounding of the waters so close to their ears.

Charlie's hat, whirling uncannily in the troubled waters, spun along the surface until it was drawn into the eddying water in the southern inlet. A wavelet pushed it against the trailing foliage of a weeping willow, and there it stayed, lightly trapped and untouched by subsequent bullets fired at it from long range.

Charlie held on to the leg, turned over in the water and was washed close against the grey. Such was the force of the water and the pressure upon the man in the saddle that the booted leg which was Charlie's lifeline came out of the stirrup and trailed alongside of the struggling horse.

There were instructions which Jim could have given at that stage, but now he was so tired that he could not raise a shout. He held on tenaciously, his biceps almost locked with strain, and gently punched the back of the grey's neck to exhort it to a last tremendous effort.

The stallion responded. Jim's trapped leg was forced against its flank. He had neglected to remove his spurs on entry, and now the weight on that right leg pushed a rowel against the grey body. In pain, it lashed out with a hind leg. This powerful motion had the effect of knocking Charlie away from the leg.

He called out hoarsely and unheard, clawed for something else to catch hold of, and, purely by chance, he grabbed the stallion's tail. He held on to his last chance and in that position, strung out almost to his full five and a half feet, he was slowly drawn ashore, trailing behind the horse and rider.

Bullets from the mesa peppered the frothing inlet as the grey slithered, bucked and finally began to haul itself clear. Jim, for one, knew what the new sort of hail was all about, but, after his recent buffeting by the punishing river waters, the new hazard seemed trivial and out of context.

He slipped out of the saddle almost before solid earth was under his feet. The grey climbed to higher ground and he was able to get a grip around Charlie's waist and disentangle him from the beast which was more than tired of the strain on its sensitive appendage.

With Charlie's feet not making much of an impression upon the slope, they slowly mounted to drier and higher ground, trailing their watery excesses behind them, and knowing some slight pleasure from the feel of solid earth and the caress of ferns and grasses.

'We made it, amigo,' Jim croaked gratefully.

Beside him, Charlie made a noise which needed a lot of interpretation. At the top of the slope and in the protecting shadow of drooping water-side trees, they made an effort to straighten up. Each still rested a hand upon the shoulder of the other.

Jim was already beginning to feel something of a mild renewal of energy, or was it just relief at being spared by the waters? Charlie, on the other hand, looked drained and strained, as if he had been half-drowned and would never be the same person again. His overbright eyes appeared to be searching Jim's soul, almost as though he had not seen him before.

Jim smiled, thinking it would bring his partner comfort, but Charlie only looked away. The stronger man had to sit his partner at the foot of a tree bole and leave him there while he did one or two small things to further their ends.

Miraculously, three small cigars and a few matchsticks, carried over inside Jim's hat, had remained dry. Jim struck a match, lighted two cigars, drew on them and poked one between Charlie's lips. Charlie's expression did not relax. Once again he appeared to have suffered a permanent water change. He knew what the cigar was for, however, because he began to draw on it without any apparent conscious effort.

Somewhat reassured, Jim moved away and dragged his tired limbs for the time it took to build a small fire. That done, he lighted it and sat down near it on the opposite side to Charlie. He gave Charlie a wave, explained that he was tuckered out, and promptly shuffled himself into a position for sleep. All he had the energy to do was remove his hat and his jacket.

In spite of the wetness of his clothing, he was slipping away into an exhausted sleep before the fire threw out any heat.

★　★　★

The flames of the fire drew Charlie's strange gaze away from Jim's slumped figure. The waters of the Rio Grande, and the blow on the head from the river rock, had undone the damage which the earlier gun wound had done to his brain.

The proper reason for his strained, withdrawn expression was the return of his memory. He was seeing Jim Bayles for the first time as one of the other side, one of the law-abiding. One of those his father had always counselled not to trust. *Never trust an honest man, Charlie,* he used to say, *it'll always get you into trouble.*

Jason Garnett had been against the law and those who kept it for all his days. He came of good Garnett stock, if you could call Garnett stock good. And yet in spite of his code of living he had not been a successful lawbreaker.

Charlie pushed aside feelings about his father. He glanced through the mounting smoke at the shadowed face of the man his father would have despatched rather than trust. Jim Bayles. Jim Bayles was the man who had jumped the Garnett boys in far-off Ghost Town Creek!

He was the man — the only one

possible — who had stopped him, Charlie Garnett, with a head wound which had all but killed him. And here he was, asleep on this alien river bank and just waiting to receive whatever a vengeful outlaw should decide to hand out to him. More and more clear and almost incredible thoughts flashed through Charlie's brain.

Jim had fought the Garnetts on more than one occasion. In fact, due to the head injury for which he was responsible, he had made him — Charlie — fire on his own kith and kin!

Automatically, he reached for his revolvers. They were both in the right place, in the holsters. And yet the river had given them a good soaking. Maybe they wouldn't fire properly until they had had treatment and a chance to dry out.

But there was still the knife. In their way, the Garnetts were all skilled with the knife. Charlie thought over what he had been told about the knife murders in Casagrande. If the Garnett pride needed re-establishing, those killings would do it more than anything else.

Charlie stood up, feeling a little unsteady on his feet. While he toyed with the knife alongside the fire, and stared down at his riding companion, all the noises caused by the river came up at him again. He remembered how he had suffered in the extremity of fear, both before and after his head came into contact with the rock.

Jim, undeniably, had been working for all he was worth to make sure that they both got safely across. Maybe he ought to be spared for a few hours longer on account of that effort.

Jason Garnett would not have approved a stay of execution: but he was not a man much looked up to in outlaw circles. Jason had spent too much time in jail for the other branch of the family to care a lot for him. He had actually died behind bars, and Charlie had gone in fear of him until the news of his death had been told. Jason's failures in life accounted for

Charlie being the odd-man-out among his cousins.

On this occasion, when he was trying to marry the immediate past to the present, he permitted himself to know that he hated Matt and the other two almost as much as he had hated his father.

He toyed with the knife, pressing its sharp point against the tip of his thumb. Jim slept on, and Charlie felt weary. His bloody-mindedness, reborn with the recovery of his memory, faded for the time being. He knew how lonely it would be on that stretch of Mexican soil with only the body of a former partner for company.

He put the knife back in its sheath, shrugged his shoulders in Jim's direction and slowly hauled off his soaked shirt. He held his garments towards the flames, but he had slumped to the ground and fallen asleep again before they were dry.

15

The noises of the river which had threatened death had the effect of lulling them into a deep sleep when exhaustion took over. Any other hazard during that night would have found both of them wanting, but none came to disturb their slumber.

In the morning, the sun was slow to get through to them and make known the arrival of the new day on account of the thick foliage in the basin strip of the Little Bend.

Nearly fifteen minutes had gone by during which each of them had been drowsily awake before either felt the need to make contact. At first, when they rose to their feet and stretched, their concern was for their soaked clothes and the weapons.

Their clothes had born the marks of the trail before the river water hit them.

Through the night they had partially dried, but they would never look quite as good again. Side by side, they worked to boost the dead fire and when it was sparking with life again a brief period of indecision ended with their walking through to the steep sloping bank and gazing into the water which had all but denied them the right to cross.

'I've seen it before, Charlie, but I still find myself wonderin' where all that volume of water comes from. Makes ordinary men like us seem mighty unimportant, doesn't it?'

'It sure does, Jim,' Charlie replied morosely. 'Rather than attempt to recross that river in the same way, I'd take any alternative. Still, that may not be necessary. Ain't no signs of the enemy yet. Probably that means that the nearest ford or ferry is a few miles away. What do you propose to do now?'

'We take a quick look up and down our side of the water. Eat breakfast and then make our way inland. I don't suppose the Mexican *rurales* will patrol this part of the Little Bend very often. After all, only fools or men hard pressed would attempt a crossin' in such a spot.'

'I agree with you. But we should move on. By tales I've heard, the Mexican police are not like ours. We might not get as far as the nearest *rurales* post if they took a dislike to us. Was your brother, Heck, a good swimmer?'

Jim frowned. 'I guess he was, but he wouldn't have crossed here unless he was in trouble.'

Charlie gave him a long look. He agreed exactly with Jim's statement, but he refrained from mentioning that trouble comes in all shapes and sizes.

Although they ached, on account of their previous night's exertions, their scratch breakfast went down well. A brief examination of the horses, which had not wandered far, showed that there was no need for any delay on their account.

As they mounted up, Charlie looked to be bursting with questions, but he did not put any. Jim was grateful not to have to answer any because he now had no clear idea of where to start looking. He was in a foreign country which had fought a war with his own in his lifetime.

He was perplexed. Gradually, the grey moved ahead to a distance of about five yards. The heavy growth of grass, fern, scrub and trees persisted for quite a good distance, although they thought they were heading directly away from the river.

It was inevitable that Jim's thoughts should go back to the violent and disturbing events of the previous few days. These were not really the sort of incidents that he would have wanted to write down either.

After a time, he slowed down and indicated by a gesture that he wanted Charlie to overtake him.

'Charlie, the findin' of that corpse, the remains of Wilbur Dyce, came as something of a shock to me. How do you see it, in the light of what we've been tryin' to find out?'

Charlie was slow to answer. He knew that Jim still thought his memory was not functioning. He could have given a rather shocking reply, but perhaps because he had spent so much time in the young journalist's company, he was tactful.

'I don't think Dyce died a natural death. I don't think you do, either. So, he was killed. He must have been killed because someone wanted to get away from him, to escape. Or perhaps he was killed because he had found something valuable. Do I make sense, Jim?'

'You do, amigo. What we need to know is who killed him and for why. If he went to that spot with my brother, then my brother — if he's still alive — has some explainin' to do.'

Charlie coughed. 'It's no good burdenin' yourself with guilt over what happened to Dyce. You have to stick to the same idea that brought you out of the United States, that your brother is missin' an' you need to find him for your own peace of mind. If you don't achieve peace of mind, Hector Bayles might as well stay buried in the past!'

Without being aware of it, Charlie had summed up the main issue quite succinctly. Jim appreciated what he had said, and he turned in the saddle to take a close look at him and to register his profound approval.

It was while he had his back turned and his attention upon Charlie that disaster struck. The two riders were in the last twenty yards of the thick belt of growth along the basin. Without being aware of it, they rode almost into the midst of seven Mexican riders who had planted themselves among the fringe trees and remained quite still.

'Lift your hands, *gringos!*'

Jim contrived to move the grey a few feet to one side as he raised his hands. Charlie, however, was no better placed, and he at once saw that this was a time for discretion rather than futile valour.

He slowly raised his hands while his eyes were still busy.

'I think I have become too old for the job of bodyguard, Jim, or perhaps on Mexican soil it requires a different sort of man!'

'Don't let it bother you, Charlie. It was my fault entirely. I wasn't even lookin' the way we were going. This, I suppose, puts us in the hands of the local police. A new experience for me.'

Apart from the man who had called the order, all the other mounted Mexicans sat their horses like statues for upwards of a minute. All of them wore tall, widebrimmed unadorned hats. Two were definitely heavy enough to be in serious trouble without a broad belt. One was obviously old for that kind of work, and three young men were devoid of facial hair, except for their eyebrows.

'My name is Sanchez. I am givin' the orders. My men will take your weapons an' you will do strictly what you are told. You are trespassing.'

Sanchez had moved forward some five yards. He had done it carefully so as not to get between his men and the two prisoners. He was a tough-looking domineering fellow who differed from the others inasmuch as his moustache was brown rather than the customary black.

The old man and one of the fat riders came forward and took the guns. They did it efficiently, removing the revolvers first and then the shoulder weapons. Jim turned in his saddle to see how Charlie was reacting to the reversal. The latter turned and twisted but only from the hips upwards. He was not about to do anything that might earn a bullet.

He murmured: 'I don't think I'll be goin' abroad in a hurry after this. That is, if we survive this encounter.'

Jim chuckled in spite of his forebodings, and shortly after that the riders, now boosted to nine on account of the prisoners, removed themselves from the thick belt of growth by riding further inland. Within minutes, over rolling hill slopes, they got their first sighting of cultivated land.

Two extensive meadows on an adjacent hill had been ploughed and used for crops. Sanchez skirted between the two of them, followed closely by his prisoners who were sided by watchful riders on each flank and a single guard at the rear.

The building they were heading for puzzled Jim. Its immediate lands were enclosed by a stone wall which had been painted white. To him it was inconceivable that a *rurales* staging post should hold so much ground.

The track ran alongside the wall after a time, and the party came to a halt near an ornate iron gate arched in stone. A tall, lean man on the other side started to smile until he saw the prisoners. The sight of them caused his expression to change. He opened the gates with haste and stood back, wondering if there had been any shooting.

Sanchez manoeuvred his horse to one side and allowed two others to go ahead. Inside the wall, buildings of various sorts, the kind associated with a big ranch and farm, were scattered over a wide area, but the only building which took Jim's fancy was the big sprawling hacienda with the green tiles and shutters.

Sanchez grinned, seeing Jim's interest. 'Take a good look at the ranch house, *gringo*. I don't think you will ever see the inside of it.'

But Jim's gaze had shifted to another point of interest as two well-groomed animals, a white mare and a black stallion, came around the corner of the building, led by a mounted groom on a lean skewbald.

There was a peal of female laughter and immediately following it a beautiful young woman with raven-black hair came out of the hacienda in a big cream hat and a white shirt worn loosely at the waist over a grey riding skirt. She toyed with a short riding quirt, and seemed surprised when Sanchez bowed in the saddle and indicated the prisoners.

While the young woman waited at the top of the gallery steps, a man followed her out of doors. He pulled up even more quickly, and then came down the steps to find out what had been happening. While Sanchez explained things in rapid, elided Spanish, the newcomer's restless eyes went over the two prisoners taking in every detail. At the same time, Jim and Charlie were every bit as active.

They saw before them a man of about thirty years, dressed like a rich Spaniard or Mexican, with a touch of lace at the neck and cuffs, and a short tailored bolerostyle black jacket in keeping with his tight pants and black cylindrical hat which had a straight brim and flat top. The scarlet sash at the waist was also Mexican in style, but the way two holstered six-shooters were strapped beneath it seemed more like north of the border.

There was something familiar about

the full face and the long straight nose and the pale blue eyes, and Jim wondered if the sun had affected his brain, or the river had given him hallucinations, because he was trying to put his missing brother's characteristics on this totally foreign Mexican.

And yet the fellow had a way of standing that was reminiscent of Heck, and when he did hand gestures there was something familiar about that, too. The woman danced down the steps, piqued about being kept waiting. The mounted groom held the mare while she mounted herself, and still her escort did not come.

The sideburns were just as thick, although they were trimmed in a different fashion. Suddenly, Jim was convinced. He started his mount going forward. Two of the guards at once raised their rifles, but the man in the dude outfit went against Sanchez's sharp order, and Jim was allowed to advance.

For a few moments the two regarded

each other while Jim was still mounted, and then their expressions changed.

Jim remarked: 'No wonder I couldn't find you all this time. You've changed your appearance quite a bit, an' I was lookin' in the wrong country!'

Hector gave out with that big gusty chuckle of his, and his deep chest swelled under the bolero coat. 'Hell an' tarnation, brother, you're supposed to be a writer, not an investigator. You took I don't know what kinds of risks pushin' your way into Mexican territory like this! Why, only last week three outlaws, let me see, Hickstead, Bruce an' another fellow, came over and had a run in with the *rurales*.

'They made the mistake of drawin' an' shootin' like they'd been brought up to by the Garnett boys, an' now all they have to commemorate them are three wooden crosses! Still, that's another story an' you're here.

'We have to talk, but right now I have to go on a visit to my wife's father's place. You could rest up here, an' we can talk when I get back. Maybe the introductions will be better then, when you've had a chance to clean up a little and get over your unexpected reception.'

At that moment, Jim felt nothing but relief. He dismounted as though all his troubles were over and warmly embraced the brother he had thought to be dead. They shook hands until their arms ached and Charlie was embarrassed.

Jim broke off at last, raised his hat to the young Spanish woman and pointed to his partner. 'This is Charlie Crease, my ridin' pardner an' friend. Without Charlie I would never have made it here. You go about your business, Heck, an' — like you said — we'll talk when you get back. All we need at the moment is a place to sleep in an' a wash-room. The Rio Grande gave us a bad crossin'.'

Heck spread his arms in a thoroughly Latin manner. He explained that a mistake had been made; that his own brother had arrived, and that the newcomers were to be given anything they required in his absence.

Some of the guards beamed. One of them shook hands with Charlie, and only Sanchez, a former member of the *rurales*, found it difficult to show the change of outlook. Jim and Charlie stood on the steps and waved while those who were going horse-riding went out of sight.

After that, Sanchez turned them over to a buxom Mexican woman with an air of authority, who took them down a tiled corridor to a spare room with a double bed. They were shown the bathroom adjoining, and a bottle of wine was sent in to them before they were allowed to rest.

Side by side, they soaked their tired bodies in twin tubs and smoked Spanish cigars. After a while, Jim tried a little conversation.

'This hacienda is a far cry from that buildin' at Waterend. He might have been dead, an' now he's very much alive. But with all these riches I still don't feel right about him. I believe you will know why. In case my conscience ever gets troubled, I'm glad I still have you, Charlie.'

'I'm glad you still have me, amigo,' Charlie murmured, but he did not explain his reasons for agreeing.

16

Over dinner that evening, Dona Anita Bayles (the Mexican did not pronounce the name at all like the American way) showed that she was a good conversationalist. She chattered about this and that in American and in Spanish, played on a mandolin brought along by a servant, and acted as a good hostess and a wife.

She was showing off her upbringing, being the daughter of one Don Sebastian, who lived across the valley to the south in an even bigger hacienda. Her curvaceous body was displayed well in a low-cut bottle-green evening gown. A gold necklace hung about her long neck, and several combs which twinkled with small jewels held her long dark tresses in place on the back of her head.

One Mexican in a white coat brought

and served the food and wine. Two women helped him in the kitchen and the dining-room, and the long dining-table, centrally placed in a room with beams and an open fireplace at one end, had only four diners, the master, the mistress and the two guests.

Jim mellowed under the influence of the good wine, even though he knew there were difficult times ahead since this encounter. Charlie, whose mind picked up every bit of new knowledge with ease since it was restored, watched and listened, and talked when manners demanded it.

He felt that Hector might have an idea of his true identity and he wondered how Jim would sort out that little difficulty when the feasting was over and the discussion had to take place. The meal and the pleasantries came to an end about half past nine.

The Senora, Heck's wife, withdrew to her bedroom shortly afterwards and the men were left to their cigars and their own devices. They strolled about in the room next to the dining-room. Hector was in an expansive mood.

'How would you like to stay in Mexico for good, Jim?' he queried, beaming all over his face.

'I don't think I could do that, and in any case there are things we have to discuss like the present and the past, before we can think about the future. Why don't we take a stroll right now, an' clear up a few points about what went before all this? We could stroll outside the walls of your domain, on neutral ground, if you like to call it that.'

Hector glanced hard at Jim's expression. He then took a critical look at Charlie, but his outlook appeared to be quite neutral.

'All right, then, we stroll out of doors. Your friend, Charlie, as he knows, can go anywhere he wants. Maybe he ought to leave us alone for a short while, though. If he doesn't mind.'

Charlie shrugged. 'I'm goin' to our room, anyways. So I'll see you later.'

He left them, and they wandered out into the open and across the kitchen garden. They traversed a vineyard and soon came to a small wooden door in the wall. Jim stepped through it and Hector followed him. In the shade of trees they came to a halt, facing each other.

'All right, Jim, what is it you really need to know before you can fully enjoy my hospitality?'

Jim nodded and flicked an inch of ash off his cigar. 'Why did you have to drop out of circulation when that big drive against the Garnetts was on, Heck? An' why did you set yourself up over this side of the border without tryin' to get in touch?'

The former federal officer gripped and twisted his cigar with rather more pressure than was necessary. For a long time, he had dreaded questions like these and, coming from his own brother, they seemed all the more difficult to answer.

'It's a long story. You see, I changed

my identity to some extent when I crossed the Rio Grande. You can see how it is over here. Things are different.'

'You can't avoid the explanations, Heck. I've been searchin' for you for a long time. I've had trouble on my back trail so long I think almost like an outlaw. Like a man on the run!'

'Are you quite certain about that hombre who rides with you, Jim, because for my money he has the Garnett cast of feature. I'd be very careful, if I were you. I could have him removed quite quietly if you wanted him out of the way. That's one thing I could do for you.'

'Charlie Crease has been a good bodyguard for me, Heck, an' he mustn't be interfered with in any way. Do you understand that? Now, let's get back to the past. To Waterend, for instance, an' the body of a man named Wilbur Dyce. What can you tell me about him?'

Heck's bold face looked troubled.

239

'Dyce, who would he be?'

Jim's control suddenly snapped. He swung a punch at Heck which caught the latter on the side of his jaw and threw him back against a tree bole. Heck lost his cigar, but instead of grabbing it out of the grass straight away or throwing a punch, he tensed up and listened.

This angered Jim even more, so that he glanced around at the wall and the trees at his back. 'If you've got any of that private army of yours hangin' around here while we talk, you've really sunk low, little brother!'

'There was no call to say that, Jim. I don't have anybody listenin', but I did think for a minute there was someone hangin' around.'

He retrieved his cigar and asked what they had been talking about. Even after the terrible river crossing, Jim felt that he was still a match for his heavily muscled brother, but he wanted to hear some answers before he worked off his pent-up anger on him.

'Dyce was a posse rider who came away from the rest, in your company. He died at Waterend, and no one knew where he was buried until Charlie and I found him. My own view is that you decided to disappear right after Wilbur died, an' he didn't die a natural death. So talk.'

'*That*'s what's botherin' you! You think I killed him in cold blood! That's why you're actin' up instead of actin' like a true brother.'

'Waterend was the place where one of the Garnetts, since deceased, buried the loot they took from the Western Settlers Association. I believe the loot was buried in the spot which is now Dyce's burial place. Am I right?'

Hector worked to get that distant troubled look out of his face as Jim cautiously advanced on him.

'Dyce an' me, we found the loot like you said, buried there in that old cellar. When we turned it up it gave us both a surprise. Dyce must have had the idea of winnin' it all for himself. He went

241

out for something an' when he came back there was a short pause. Pure instinct made me duck sideways. A bullet missed my neck by less than an inch. As it happened, I dived towards my gun belt. I pulled a six-gun and shot him dead. And that's the truth! After that, I panicked, what with the money bein' there an' all. I didn't think anyone would believe my version of the story. So I buried him. It took me a long time to pull that rottin' floor out an' bury him under beaten earth, but I did it, an' after that I avoided all the others in the search an' came south of the border. You should be able to guess the rest. I'm still surprised that you should be the one to find me after all this time.'

'Didn't you think that ties of blood might keep me searchin' after everybody else had given up? And that missin' loot has put the Garnetts back on trail, as well. You may have to deal with them after we've gone.'

'You — you're leavin', Jim? You're goin' to leave things as they are?'

'There's jest the matter of the Bayles family conscience an' the Western Settlers money. That's all. I don't think I could stay here, knowin' what you'd done with it, Heck. So get that amount of money together somehow, an' tomorrow I'll take it away with me.'

'It — it might be a little difficult returnin' it without havin' to answer a lot of awkward questions,' Heck ventured.

'But I'll answer them, jest the same, Heck, so don't try to put me off! My conscience isn't as easy to fool as yours!'

'All right, Jim! I understand!' Heck stepped forward with his hand raised. He laid it gently against Jim's chest. 'I have the amount in the house, an' the way it is it won't be difficult for you to carry. It's the least I can do, to give it back to those who lost it in the first place. Your conscience is good for me, too, Jim. Now, let's go back in the house.'

Jim felt reasonably sure that Hector

would keep his word, but he could not help feeling angry when his brother sought to smooth things over or to minimise his earlier crime. After all, a man who had used somebody else's capital and made a personal fortune wouldn't miss it any more when his riches were established.

Although he condescended to shake hands when they got back to the house, Jim immediately left Heck and went to the room he shared with Charlie. Charlie, to his surprise, came in afterwards. As they stripped and prepared for bed, Charlie discarded one of his twin revolvers and the sight of it brought Jim's thoughts away from Hector and back to his alliance with Charlie.

'Don't tell me you've been carryin' out your bodyguard's duties even here?' he remarked, in a surprised tone of voice.

Charlie shrugged and then nodded. 'I was over there, anyways. Heck heard me move up on the wall. There was a time when Charlie Garnett had the upper hand over Charlie Crease an' I might have shot Hector an' maybe you, too. But something about the way you handled him cooled me off, so I didn't have to use my gun.'

Jim groaned. 'You must have recovered your memory after that bang on the head in the river. I'm glad you heard what you did. I'd hate to have to repeat all that to anyone. And thanks for not retaliatin' straight away when you found yourself with a man who had shot you in the head.'

Charlie nodded in the semi-darkness. 'I don't know how it'll be in future,' he confessed. 'I have these warrin' thoughts in my head pullin' me this way an' that. It's as well you know what you're up against, 'cause I don't feel I'm the master of myself any more.'

'I've tried to control your destiny for too long, Charlie. I'll take a chance on the future.'

Neither of them was able to sleep for a long time, but Jim, eventually, was the first to achieve it.

17

The parting, surprisingly enough, was not as difficult as Jim had thought it might be. Hector appeared to be in the best of spirits over breakfast. He had already intimated that his brother and the other guest would be leaving after the meal.

The grey and the pinto had been well groomed and lightly fed before the journey, and Sanchez was the one to bring them around to the front gallery and to offer his services as a guide to the nearest river ferry, some two or three miles downstream towards the south-east.

At last, it was time for the two travellers to move away.

Hector drew his brother apart for a while and handed over to him a small leather valise. He opened it briefly and showed what it contained. 'The weight of this won't get you down, brother. Take a look see. Small bars of gold, and quite a few precious stones of fine quality. I happen to know that they are the equivalent in value of the original Western Settlers cash. You see, I always intended to hand it over . . . '

Hector's explanation tailed off because of the intensity of Jim's gaze. They shook hands, the thanks were said, and the two men mounted up. Hector came along with them as far as the big gate, explaining as he walked how to get to the ferry, as they had refused the guide.

'If you ever feel like comin' back again, Jim, you'll be welcome,' Heck assured him.

Jim thanked him again. It was clear by his manner that he had no intention of returning. They both knew it. As they hesitated over a parting that they both felt deeply, Charlie raised his hat and that had the effect of breaking the tension. Side by side, the two riders went through the gate. Hector himself closed the entrance after them. There seemed to be an air of finality about the way he did it, although he stayed behind the gates and stared after them until they were out of sight.

Within half an hour they were on the winding, undulating path just up from the river bank, riding one behind the other.

'You want to take a look at ten thousand dollars' worth of valuables on their way back to the United States, Charlie?' Jim called back unhappily.

'Are you talkin' to Garnett or Crease?' Charlie asked calmly.

'Only you can answer that, pardner. I'd hate to lose you, though, so soon after losin' a brother.'

Jim closed his saddle pocket again and they proceeded in silence. Every now and then they caught sight of the river in brief glimpses. Their fears occasioned by that other horrifying crossing were never far from the surface. Neither of them wanted to pause for a long look, until a stop was necessary.

Another hour later, they got their first distant glimpse of the flat, barge-like cross-river ferry. Between tall trees on either bank stout ropes ran through pulleys to prevent the current taking charge and sending the sluggish boat down-river to the confluence with the Pecos. Four long side-oars and another used at the stern minimised the hard work occasioned by pulling on the ropes.

It was a difficult means of crossing, but it worked, and not many people used it, except for shifting cattle occasionally.

At the break in the trees from which it was visible, Jim took the opportunity of slackening and rocking his saddle and taking a drink, but he had no interest in the distant ferry and so he did not take the spyglass. Charlie, by contrast, gave the ferry and the banks on either side a very thorough study before he was satisfied with his observations.

When they had moved on a little way,

Charlie spoke up. 'You haven't forgotten we may have to deal with my cousins again soon?'

Jim yawned. He seemed to be feeling more than just ordinary tiredness. 'Okay, okay, Charlie. But don't let's anticipate trouble yet. We haven't left the foreign country, remember.'

Charlie allowed the conversation to flag. Some two hundred yards from the landing stage, which was merely a well-trodden flat section of river bank, he invigorated his mount and overtook.

'If it's all the same to you, I'd like you to ride down to the ferry alone. What do you say?'

Jim managed a tired grin. 'There was another time when you withdrew an' I thought the worst, but I was wrong. Do it your way, Charlie. I owe you a few favours, anyway.'

* * *

The barge looked for all the world like a section of landing stage. Three horses were tied to posts along one side and their owners, enveloped in ponchos and steeple hats, looked as if they had been asleep on the deck all night.

Jim's grey clattered on to the boards with a noise which would have awoken the dead. He rode the animal up to the forward end, hitched it to a post and casually dismounted. He walked back towards the sleepers, wondering if they had anything to do with the crew. A momentary flash of interest in Charlie's progress took his attention and, when he looked again, all three Mexicans had rolled to one side, very much on the alert, and were pointing revolvers at him.

'Good day, señores.'

Matt Garnett came to his feet slowly, chuckled when he heard the Spanish name, and gestured with one of his weapons for the other two to close in upon the prisoner.

'So, our Mr Bayles has been abroad long enough to know a little of the language. Nice to see you on the way home again. Toss down your gun.'

Jim did as he was told. He knew he was in the tightest fix of his life and yet he did not seem to react that way. It was as if his faculties had clammed up on him; as if he had seen too much conflict in too short a time.

'Wouldn't you rather talk about the loot which was lost to you for so long, Matt?' he asked conversationally. 'I have it here in this small case.'

He made as if to open it, but there was a chorus of protest from all three outlaws. He studied their faces closely for the first time. Matt, with his sparse auburn beard and moustache. Lee's distinctive ginger moustache, and the fleshy pockmarked face of the green-eyed one known as Drag.

'You're afraid I might have a stick of dynamite in it, or a loaded weapon?' Jim spat at them.

He glared at each one in turn before lowering the case to the deck and pushing it towards them with his foot.

Side by side, they came forward, inch

by inch. The pull of treasure was not dead in them. Jim raised his hands. He backed away as they advanced. None of them seemed to see anything significant in his movement.

'All right, Drag, you go forward an' open it, but don't make the mistake of gettin' in the line of fire, 'cause if so you won't live to share it!'

Drag, who had been rather shaken by Matt's words, was just about to reach for the fastenings when a voice from ashore made him hesitate.

'Ho, there! Can you boys hear me?'

Matt whistled soundlessly. 'That's Charlie's voice. He didn't perish in the river. He's back in business.'

'This is Charlie! Jason's boy! I'm tellin' you to stand up an' back away from that valise! I'm goin' to start shootin' at it any time!'

'You're bluffin', Charlie,' Matt called back. 'Come on down here an' take a quarter share. You can't fool us, we've known you too well.'

Drag was feeling a twinge in his old

hip wound, the one he attributed to Charlie. He was not quite clear whether Matt intended to bring Charlie back into the reckoning. Avarice made him stretch his fingers to the fastenings again, and that started the shooting.

Charlie's first accurate rifle bullet went through Drag's right arm. All three of his cousins then knew that he meant business, whatever the state of his mind. While the echo of the shot went around the banks of the river, Jim ran back to the edge of the barge and dived into the river. All three of his enemies wanted to run to the edge and pump shells at him, but such was the menace ashore that they did not have the time or the immediate inclination. He plunged deep and came up grasping the rough side of the barge not far from the restless legs of the horse, through which he had dived.

The sound of many shots hitting woodwork and other targets boomed around in his head. It seemed endless, and then it did stop. In the silence which followed, he waited for the searchers, but none came. Eventually, he heaved himself up, risking a shot, and saw that all three Garnetts were out of action on the deck.

Getting out of the water with its tugging current was a slow job. He found Drag stretched out on his back, shot through the head. Lee had been hit in the chest and the abdomen, while Matt had absorbed no less than three bullets before succumbing with his head and shoulders over the side, in the water.

All Jim's feeling then was for Charlie. He failed to answer two spirited calls, but eventually his pinto came plodding down the approach track with him riding rather loosely. He rode straight on to the barge, noted how the bodies had fallen, and saw that the valise was still where Jim had left it.

They stood and faced each other, a few feet apart, two tired men who had seen an awful lot of carnage and who sought only peace for the future. After a time, the restlessness of the horses helped them to get into action.

'Will you be seekin' bounty for these bodies, Jim?'

'No, I don't want any bounty, Charlie. Let's tidy up an' be on our way.'

In spite of his words, Jim, himself, was the one to dump the bodies over the side for purposes of river disposal. Charlie watched him without emotion, and gave himself the task of untying the barge. For two men, it was hard work manoeuvring it across. Half-way over they paused for breath.

'Jim, do you reckon you could do with me around all the time? Permanently?'

'I reckon I could. In fact, I'm so used to havin' you around all the time I might not be able to write properly if you went off on your own. Stick around, by all means, Charlie. You're all the kin I need.'

'Now that's a darned funny thing, Jim. You put words to my thoughts.

You're all the kin I need, too. Jest one thing, though. What if some smart hombre ever came along an' insisted I was Charlie Garnett instead of Charlie Crease?'

'Then I'd have to explain how he was wrong, wouldn't I?'

'An' if he wouldn't be told?' Charlie probed gently.

'Then I'd have to take on as bodyguard, for a change. If the worst came to the worst, we could always backtrack into Mexico, at least for a spell.'

Charlie hoped never to visit Mexico again, but he knew for certain that Jim would go to a great deal of trouble for him if they stayed together, and what had been said fully satisfied him.

Working as a team, they propelled the barge across to the Texas side. Shortly before they arrived, Jim moved the treasure valise to a less obvious place.

Books by David Bingley
in the Linford Western Library:

THE BEAUCLERC BRAND
ROGUE'S REMITTANCE
STOLEN STAR
BRIGAND'S BOUNTY
TROUBLESHOOTER ON TRIAL
GREENHORN GORGE
RUSTLERS' MOON
SUNSET SHOWDOWN
TENDERFOOT TRAIL BOSS
HANGTOWN HEIRESS
HELLIONS' HIDEAWAY
THE JUDGE'S TERRITORY
KILLERS' CANYON
SIX-SHOOTER JUNCTION
THE DIAMOND KID
RED ROCK RENEGADES
HELLIONS AT LARGE
BUZZARD'S BREED
REDMAN RANGE
LAWMAN'S LAMENT
THE COYOTE KIDS
BRIGAND'S BLADE
SILVER CREEK TRAIL

OWLHOOT BANDITS
KILLER'S CREEK
LOPEZ'S LOOT
COWTOWN KIDNAP

Other titles in the
Linford Western Library:

SHOOT, RUN OR DIE!

Jake Douglas

Cody had once fought a cougar to a standstill — bare-handed. He's not a man to mess with. When Curtin and Willis rob him, leave his partner parboiled and burn down the cabin, there is nowhere for the killers to hide. Now a whole town want him for their sheriff — all but Deputy Blake Ross. He makes more trouble for Cody than he's ever seen, enough to plant him on Boot Hill with men he had hunted and killed.

IRON EYES MAKES WAR

Rory Black

The infamous bounty hunter Iron Eyes is forced to chase down Joe Brewster, the wanted outlaw, into an arid desert, despite being badly wounded in a showdown with Brewster's brothers. When he loses his pony, he follows on foot and discovers an oasis in a valley. He finds that families are living there under threat of death by Don Miguel Sanchez and his army of vaqueros. Will Iron Eyes leave, or will he fight until the bloody showdown?

McRAE'S LAST TRAIL

Terry Murphy

He's badly wounded and trailed by Durell, the ruthless bounty hunter, but Maury McRae reaches the town of Gray's Flat and is nursed back to health by the beautiful Heather Cordell . . . In need of a fast gun, ruthless rancher Max Nelson has offered McRae much-needed work. Unfortunately though, this involves a serious threat to Heather and her brother. McRae's in a dilemma — his situation seems hopeless. Then the dream fades away as a highly dangerous situation develops . . .

RUSTLER'S RANGE

Billy Hall

Tad Strong's bold attempt to capture the outlaw king in his own domain, and make his escape, had gone badly wrong. In retreat, he was propped against the wall; pinned down, surrounded, and hopelessly outnumbered. Overwhelmed by the constant barrage of bullets and splintering wood — he was doomed. At least he would die thinking of Becky . . . He'd failed to complete his mission. Now, all he could do was to wait for the final bullet . . .

THE BATTLE FOR SKILLERN TRACT

Matt Laidlaw

Zac Hunter's plan to rob the Nacogdoches bank goes awry: the bank is already in the midst of a robbery and Marshal Dan McCrae is dying from gunshot wounds. Then he's offered McCrae's job and forced to serve notice on businessmen drilling for oil on the Skillern tract. With many factions in Nacogdoches struggling for supremacy, Hunter becomes embroiled in a cycle of treachery and murder. The showdown will culminate in a blazing gunfight on the Skillern tract.

WAITING FOR THE HANGMAN

Carlton Youngblood

When Buck Armstrong agrees to take on the job of protecting a friend's friend, he has to accompany Vanessa Grange who is riding on the stagecoach to visit her Uncle Clarence. Unfortunately, however, he's in jail awaiting the hangman and must pay the price for his involvement with the Henry Plummer gang. Before that happens he wants Buck to help the girl find Plummer's hidden stash of stolen gold. But there are others around who also want the gold.